Beneath
the Olive Tree

A Love Story That Never Happens...
But Changes Everything

J. D. SMITH

Scribe & Canvas Publishing
South Carolina

Paperback ISBN: 979-8-9995975-6-4
Library of Congress Control Number: 2025944754

Published by Scribe & Canvas Publishing™
Pendleton, SC | www.scribeandcanvas.com

Interior and cover design by Elev8d Designs
Printed in the United States of America
10 9 8 7 6 5 4 3 2 1

For the ones who loved quietly—
and for those who didn't notice until the wind changed.

"If you found this page, it means you stayed long enough to notice what was buried—not to be hidden, but to be rooted."
— *From the Journal*

PREFACE

This *is not a love story in the traditional sense.*
There are no grand confessions.
No orchestras.
No endings that tie themselves neatly in ribbon.
This is a story about what remains—
The kind of love that doesn't insist.
That waits in the soil.
That lingers in silence.
That gives even when nothing is given back.
Some of these pages were written from memory.
Some from wonder.
All from a place of listening—
to the wind,
to what the roots remember,
to the ache we carry when something sacred goes unnoticed.
If you came looking for plot twists, you may not find them here.
But if you came looking for moments—
those quiet, holy pauses where breath meets memory—
you've found the right tree.
It all began with a question:
What does it mean to be remembered, even if no one speaks your name aloud?
And perhaps it ends with another:
*What if the truest love stories are the ones that never quite happened—
but changed everything anyway?*

If anything lingers after these pages, let it be this:
That love—real love—does not require witness.
It leaves no map.
Only roots.

Take your seat.
The story was waiting for you.

— *J. D. Smith*

PROLOGUE:

The Reader

It was the kind of day the wind forgot—
still and warm,
like an old hymn resting on the earth's breath.
    A thin mist hung over the hillside,
softening the trees,
blurring the edges of the path.
    The olive tree stood watch as it had for generations—
its roots deep,
its branches whispering to the sky.
    At its base, near a leaning stone and a bench
overtaken by ivy,
a journal sat.
Leather-bound.
Quiet.
Waiting.
    The traveler hadn't come searching.
She was passing through—
a plain cardigan and jeans,
a small paper sack tucked beneath her arm,
a notebook of half-finished poems in her pocket.
    She wasn't lost.
Just… unanchored.

It was the stone that caught her eye:

He loved well.

No dates. No fanfare. Just that.
She sat.
Ran her fingers along the journal's spine.
Opened it.
The first line read:

"I never intended to leave a legacy. Only a life."

The pages breathed with memory.
Somewhere behind her, the leaves stirred.
She didn't look back.
She was already reading.
And so the story begins—
not with answers,
but with a quiet man,
a bench beneath a tree,
and a love
that almost bloomed.

TABLE OF CONTENTS

The Growing

"And let us not grow weary in well-doing: for in due season we shall reap, if we faint not." — Galatians 6:9

CHAPTER ONE:

A Quiet Man

He lived in a house the color of clay after rain— soft brown with chipped corners and a roof that sighed when the wind pushed too hard. The windows were slightly crooked, like eyes too tired to pretend they hadn't seen sorrow. Yet each morning, light spilled in through the thin curtains just the same, golden and forgiving, casting halos on the wooden floors.

It was the kind of house people passed by without noticing. Not out of cruelty—just distraction. Life moved quickly elsewhere. But here, in this house, it moved at the speed of grace. The steps creaked not from neglect, but memory. The walls carried silence like a song they had learned by heart.

He rose before dawn, not out of habit, but reverence. Morning, to him, was not a chore. It was an invitation. A sacred hush before the world remembered its busyness. He greeted the day with stillness, as though afraid to wake it too abruptly. The kettle sang quietly as he poured water into the same ceramic mug he'd used for years—its handle mended with a winding gold seam from where it once cracked. He never threw things away that still had purpose. People, especially.

Sometimes, before the first sip, he would rest his hand against the wooden table—solid, worn smooth by time—and whisper a small prayer. Not for himself. For others. Always others. Names never spoken aloud, just passed from his chest to the heavens like breath on glass.

The man—whose name was forgotten by many but carried in full by God—moved slowly through the hours. Not sluggishly. Deliberately. Like someone who knew that time, like soil, could be wasted if not handled with care. He fixed hinges for widows, dug gardens for single mothers, and built shelves for those who had none but a floor. He accepted no payment, only smiles, and sometimes warm bread wrapped in linen. Once, a child gave him a drawing—stick figures beneath a tree labeled "home." He kept it tucked inside his Bible.

He was not poor, though his pockets often were. His riches were measured differently: in prayers answered, in burdens lifted, in the sound of children's laughter echoing down empty streets. In the way the old dog down the lane would limp to his porch each afternoon, resting its head against his foot like a benediction. In the birds that lingered near his window, unafraid.

Some thought him strange. Others called him too gentle, too quiet, too devout for this world. He never defended himself. He only smiled the kind of smile that comes from knowing the ground you stand on is holy, even if no one else sees it. He wore the same coat for years—not out of necessity, but familiarity. The sleeves frayed just enough to tell a story, and inside the pocket, he kept a scrap of paper with the words

"Love never demands. It invites."

He did not chase. Not status, not applause, not even love. But when it came—or seemed to—he welcomed it with the same

4

open hands he used to sow seeds in the spring. The same hands that blessed bread and repaired fences and held grief like it was something sacred, not shameful.

She arrived in summer.

Like a breeze that lingered too long at the edge of stillness, she disrupted nothing but changed everything. Her laughter caught the air like chimes on a porch that had been silent too long. She asked him about his faith, his silence, his old guitar resting in the corner with three strings and dust in its belly. She teased him about the way he always looked slightly amused, as though life had whispered a secret only he understood.

He answered slowly, deliberately, like each word was a stepping stone across a river he hadn't dared cross in years. And she listened. Not politely, but with the kind of presence that made a man believe he was not invisible. She listened the way rain listens to dry land—eager to be received.

They shared bread and long walks. Talked of grace and what it meant to be enough without earning. For a time, he believed she understood—not just his words, but the space between them. The longing. The quiet joy. The sacred ache of hope.

But some things are easily admired and rarely chosen.

She admired. But she did not choose.

And so, the chapter closes not in sorrow, but in suspense.

Because love—true love—is rarely loud when it begins. It slips in like dusk, subtle and golden, until you realize the whole sky has changed.

Chapter Two:

When Summer Sat Still

The days grew slower when she stayed. Or maybe he noticed time more—its texture, its pauses, the way sunlight stitched shadows between their footsteps. Even the wind seemed to hesitate, caught between their silence and something unspoken. The air felt softer. Like it, too, had begun to wonder what could become of two people walking without needing to arrive.

She returned often, always with a question in her eyes and warmth in her voice, like someone learning a language not with grammar, but with wonder. Her laughter found places in the house that had long gone unused. She hummed while steeping tea, wiped the windows without being asked, and once rearranged his bookshelf by color—then back by author—just to see which he'd prefer.

He left it the way she'd arranged it.

Because he liked seeing her in the space even after she left.

They never called it love.

There were no declarations, no grand confessions carved into moonlight. No crescendo. But their silences began to harmonize. Not awkward. Not empty. Just enough.

Sometimes they spoke in scriptures.

Not quoting them, but living them—him kneeling to weed her mother's flower beds, her helping him sweep the church steps before Sunday. He once found her refilling the candle oil in the sanctuary, not because she'd been asked, but because she didn't like when sacred things ran dry.

They walked to nowhere in particular, trading stories like breadcrumbs, letting the path unravel beneath them. Some days they passed entire hours talking about nothing: the shape of clouds, the way birds argue like old couples, whether hope is something you plant or something you wait for.

She asked once why he didn't want more—more money, more house, more life.

He answered, eyes fixed on the trembling leaves above,

"More of the wrong thing only makes you emptier. I'd rather be full of less."

And somehow, she understood that. Or at least, she nodded like she did.

In the evenings, he played for her—clumsy fingers strumming hymns and lullabies on the old guitar, its voice as weathered as his own. She never laughed when he missed a chord. She just listened with her head tilted slightly, like she was memorizing the way contentment sounded. Once, she fell asleep to one of his songs, her head resting on the old armrest between them, a smile tucked against her cheek.

He didn't wake her.

He simply watched.

Grateful for the moment the world paused long enough to feel like home.

Their lives brushed gently. She brought candles one day, said the scent reminded her of childhood—vanilla, clove, something nostalgic and not quite nameable. He made soup from scratch and called it a feast. They shared it in chipped bowls on the porch, legs folded under them, speaking only between spoonfuls.

Neither needed much.

That was the miracle of it.

And yet—

There were moments he noticed her glancing past him. Not away, but beyond. Toward something not present. A world still calling her name in dialects of ambition. The way her hand would rest against her wristwatch just a little longer than necessary. The way her smile sometimes drifted before it reached her eyes.

Once, while standing by the river, she asked what he dreamed of.

He smiled without hesitation.

"Peace that stays. Even when nothing else does."

She didn't answer right away.

She just stared at the water as though it might tell her what her heart wanted. As though it might hold a reflection of her she hadn't quite become yet.

He didn't press.

Love, for him, was never a pursuit.

It was an offering.

There were no photographs of them together.

Only memory: the way her fingers lingered on the chipped rim of his favorite mug, how she once wept during a thunderstorm and let him hold her without explaining why, how she whispered grace over his worn hands and called them holy.

She taught him a song once—half-hummed, half-remembered from her youth. He never asked the title. But some nights, long after she was gone, he would sing it to the garden, just softly enough to keep the memory breathing.

If this was love, it came like manna—daily, quiet, only enough for that moment.

And still, he gave thanks.

Not because he believed she would stay.

But because he knew what it meant to be seen... if only for a season.

CHAPTER THREE:
The Weight of Light Things

Some days, she stayed longer than planned.

Just one more cup of tea. Just one more hour before she returned to the noise of the world. The porch became their sanctuary—a place where light dripped through the slats in slow ribbons and the scent of rosemary clung to the air like memory. It was a borrowed stillness, the kind that doesn't ask to stay but lingers anyway.

She would sit with her feet tucked under her, cupping the chipped mug like it held more than warmth. Sometimes she'd bring a peach, bite into it slowly, juice catching the corner of her mouth. He never mentioned it. He simply handed her a cloth and turned his gaze toward the horizon, like a man too reverent to disturb beauty in its simplest form.

He began to read to her.

Not novels or lofty philosophy, but the small things he wrote in the margins of his Bible or the pages of his worn journals— prayers he never spoke aloud, thoughts too tender for the pulpit. Scribbled lines about grace, about mercy, about the ache of waiting without bitterness.

She listened like someone hearing music from behind a closed door. She smiled, sometimes even closed her eyes. And he, who had lived a life of quiet giving, felt for once that someone was drawing near—not out of need, but out of choice.

He read her a line once:

"Lord, make me a landing place, not a lifeboat. Let me hold without gripping, shelter without caging."

She asked if he'd written it for someone.

He said yes.

But didn't say who.

One afternoon, while the sky simmered with the hush of late summer, she sat cross-legged on his floor, leafing through a box of keepsakes he rarely touched. A broken watch. A folded church bulletin with a child's drawing on the back. A photograph of his parents, edges curled like they were praying. A matchbook from a roadside diner. An envelope with no address—just the word *"someday"* written across it.

She held each item like it was glass.

"This is beautiful," she whispered, cradling a stone he'd carried back from a solitary retreat.

"It's just a rock," he said.

She looked up at him then, something soft in her eyes. "Not to you."

He didn't know what to say, so he said nothing. Some silences are sacred. Some answers don't need to be explained. They only need to be honored.

That week, she brought him a tie.

It was sky blue—new, soft to the touch, folded carefully in a brown paper bag. She handed it to him like a child giving a drawing, unsure if it would be treasured or tucked away.

"For Sunday," she said, almost shyly. "Just... something different."

He held it like it was an offering.

"I haven't worn a new tie in years."

"Well," she smiled, "now you can."

He didn't tell her that he had no desire to be different. That his frayed one still carried the scent of his father's cologne and the touch of his mother's pressed hands. That the old tie had been worn at weddings, funerals, and moments too ordinary to remember but too sacred to forget. He only thanked her, as he always did—with eyes that said more than his words ever dared.

Later that evening, he hung the new tie next to the old one.

Not instead of.

Beside.

She never promised anything.

There were no whispered vows or plans written on napkins. No tentative talk of tomorrows. But still, in the quiet places of his heart, he began to make room for the thought: *Maybe she sees me. Maybe she stays.*

It wasn't a hope that bloomed loudly.

It was quieter than that.

Like rain falling on soil long thought barren.

Not rushing to grow, just glad to feel again.

The days lengthened as the season prepared to turn. Leaves trembled in their green dresses, unsure whether to let go. The evenings cooled, shadows arriving earlier, curling under the porch like cats returning home.

He noticed the subtle pauses in her goodbyes. How her gaze lingered longer down the road. How her questions turned outward—about travel, art shows, the city lights. How she wore her hair a little differently, carried herself a little taller.

They spoke once—quietly, on the porch while dusk folded itself into the hills—about leaving.

Not in arguments or ultimatums, but in soft confessions.

She said the city still called to her sometimes. Not because it offered more, but because it reminded her of who she thought she was meant to become. Noise, yes. Movement, yes. But more so—meaning. And a kind of forgetting she thought she needed.

He listened, as he always did, without interrupting. And when she fell quiet, unsure whether to ask for understanding or forgiveness, he simply offered both.

"You don't have to choose between becoming and belonging," he said. "You can still grow here. But if your heart needs to wander first... I understand."

She looked at him, eyes searching.

"You make it hard to leave."

"That's not my goal," he said, gently. "But I'd be lying if I said I hadn't started making space—for something more."

His gaze lingered on the horizon, as if the sky could carry what he wasn't quite ready to say.

"I don't want to hold you back," he added, voice steady. "But if ever you turn around... you'll still find me here."

She blinked, startled by the quiet clarity of it.

Not a plea.

Not a proposal.

But something tender resting between the two.

She didn't speak. Not right away.

Instead, she reached across the table and touched his hand—just for a moment.

"I don't know what I want yet," she admitted.

"Then I'll wait to see who you become," he said.

He didn't say he hoped it would be with him.
He didn't have to.
Because love, to him, was never possession.
It was presence.
And she was still here.
For now.

CHAPTER FOUR:

The Shift in the Stillness

It began with a dinner invitation.

Not his. Hers.

A gallery opening in the city. A friend of a friend had curated something, and someone important would be there. She hadn't planned to go, she said. But then again, she hadn't planned to stay so long in a town where the trees outnumbered the traffic lights and Sunday bells were louder than ambition.

She told him casually, over soup and cornbread.

"I think I'll go," she said, fingers dancing along the rim of her water glass. "Just for the night."

He nodded.

The spoon in his hand paused for a breath longer than it needed to.

There was a smile on his lips, but something in his eyes flickered.

"Will you be all right getting there on your own?" he asked gently.

Then, after a pause—

"Would you like company?"

She glanced up, surprised—not by the offer, but by the tenderness beneath it.

"I think… I need to do this one on my own," she said. "Just to see."

"Of course," he replied, already softening the space between them. "Then I'll keep the porch light on—just in case you miss the stars out here."

The silence that followed wasn't bitter. It wasn't even cold.

It was the kind that settles into the room like a guest you didn't expect—polite, but unwelcome. It draped itself over the table between them, soft but undeniable, like a curtain tugged halfway closed on something still unfinished.

That night, she left before the stars appeared.

Said she needed to pack, to rest, to prepare.

He walked her to her car as always, hands tucked into his sleeves. The night air had cooled, and the gravel crunched beneath their feet in a rhythm that didn't match his heartbeat. He said nothing of his ache, only smiled the same soft smile he always gave her—the one that held no expectation, only offering.

She kissed his cheek—just once, gently, like punctuation at the end of a sentence she didn't want to read aloud.

And then she drove off into the deepening dusk, taillights blinking like farewells not quite certain.

He sat on the porch for a long time after.

The sky was wide and unburdened. The crickets returned to their rhythm. The wind moved carefully through the trees, as though it, too, was unsure whether to comfort or to leave him alone.

But something in him stilled.

Not in fear. Not in anger.

In recognition.

He knew this moment. Had seen it before in other forms—the way a candle flickers before surrender, the shift in the wind before a storm gathers. Not all love ends in thunder. Some simply drifts toward silence.

He ran his fingers along the armrest of the chair she often claimed. Her shape was still there, faint and imagined—the impression of presence lingering after it's gone.

She called the next morning.

Said the city was "invigorating," that the people she met were "visionaries," that the way they spoke about life made her feel "alive in a different way."

He listened.

Smiled when she spoke.

Even laughed when she told him about a man in a velvet blazer who called his paintings "emotional architecture."

She sounded so full of color, of movement.

Like someone who had stepped into a world that vibrated on a frequency he no longer tried to tune into.

But deep inside, something folded.

Not angrily. Not bitterly. Just… folded.

Because he had seen it.

In her voice.

In the stretch between her words.

She had touched something he could not give her.

Not because he lacked it. But because she no longer needed what he offered.

The next time they met, she wore perfume. Something new. Sophisticated.

He noticed. Didn't mention it. Just opened the door like he always did.

She brought stories. Names. Ideas.

People who threw words like paint and built futures out of vision boards and signatures.

And he brought stillness.

Warm tea. Soft light. The same porch. The same hands that had once held her grief like sacred glass.

She was kind. Always kind.

But kindness isn't the same as love.

And he knew that.

She was still looking at him—but not into him.

Her gaze met his, but her spirit was elsewhere.

Already writing new chapters in a life she hadn't yet invited him to read.

And so the shift came not as betrayal, but revelation.

A quiet moment in the middle of an ordinary week, where he saw with clear eyes:

She admired his peace, but she did not crave it.

She loved his soul, but she did not choose it.

She believed in his goodness, but she was not anchored by it.

And though she cared for him deeply, she was not staying.

She was already walking toward the world she'd glimpsed—bright, brimming, and full of possibility.

A world that welcomed her with applause
and didn't ask her to live slowly.

CHAPTER FIVE:

The Last Light Between Them

The day she returned, the sky was overcast—clouds hanging low, as if heaven itself was undecided. The air smelled faintly of rain yet to fall, and the leaves along the fence clung to their stems like they were unsure of what the wind might ask of them.

She didn't call ahead.

Just appeared at his door with a soft knock and eyes that held more questions than answers.

He opened it without surprise.

He had felt her coming.

Some part of him always did.

There was something about love that lingered in the corners of silence. You could feel it in the way your chest pulled tighter during certain sunrises, or how your hands reached for tea before memory even woke up. He had woken that morning with that knowing—something was shifting again.

She stepped inside like memory—

quiet, unsure of her place in the room she used to fill with laughter. Her coat was expensive now. Her heels unfamiliar. Her perfume carried notes of a world that moved faster. But her hands still trembled when she unwrapped the scarf from her neck, and he pretended not to notice. Some kindnesses are wordless.

"I thought I'd stop by," she said.

"I'm glad," he answered.

And he was.

Even if only for the moment.

Even if it cost him.

They sat where they always did, across from one another, a chipped mug between them, and the faint ticking of the old wall clock carving time into soft slivers. The same mug she used to cradle with both hands. The same clock that had once ticked too loudly, back when the air between them was lighter.

She talked.

He listened.

The city was exciting.

The work was meaningful.

She had met people who understood things differently— artists, architects, a professor who believed color could heal the body. There were opportunities she hadn't expected. Invitations. Doors she didn't know existed, now flung wide.

Her voice was animated, but he noticed the way she looked at her lap when she spoke.

The way her thumb worried the seam of her sleeve. Not guilt. Not regret. Just the soft ache of knowing you cannot live two lives and remain whole in either.

He smiled in all the right places.

Offered no resistance.

No plea to stay.

Because real love does not beg.

It blesses—even the departure.

There was a long pause.

Not the awkward kind.

The kind that knows something sacred is nearing its close.

She looked at him then—truly looked—and something in her eyes flickered.

Grief, maybe.

Or guilt.

Or a wish that the heart could live in two places at once.

He didn't try to fill the silence.

He just let her see him—fully, freely. Not as a man who had lost, but as a man who had loved.

"I want you to know," she began, her voice soft as a prayer, "you were never not enough."

He didn't flinch.

Didn't look away.

"I know," he said.

And he did.

Not because she told him.

But because he had built his life on the knowledge that worth was not dependent on being chosen.

He had been seen by God.

And that had always been enough.

They walked outside together.

The olive tree stood silent in the yard, leaves trembling under the weight of an approaching storm. Wind curled softly around its branches, carrying the scent of coming rain and something older—like the memory of a promise never spoken aloud.

She paused beneath it, fingers trailing the bark like she was trying to memorize something she had already begun to forget. The grooves in the trunk felt warm, worn, and strangely familiar.

"I used to think peace was something you earned," she said.

He turned toward her, gentle and steady.

"Peace isn't earned. It's welcomed."

She nodded, blinking hard.

The kind of blink that holds back not just tears, but years.

Then, before the words could ruin it, she stepped forward and placed a kiss on his forehead—

quiet, reverent, final.

He closed his eyes.

Not to hold on.

But to release.

Because release is sometimes the holiest part of love.

She left without fanfare.

No dramatic turn. No tears.

Just the sound of her footsteps fading down the path and the echo of the gate clicking softly shut behind her.

He watched the sky after she disappeared.

Not to wish. Not to regret. But to breathe.

He pressed his hand briefly to his chest—right where the ache lived, steady but still—and whispered, more to God than to himself:

"Thank You… for the little while."

CHAPTER SIX:

What Remained

The morning after she left, the house did not feel empty.
It felt paused.

As if the walls themselves were holding their breath, unsure whether to exhale grief or gratitude.

The light came in slower. Not dimmer, but more diffused—like even the sun was unsure of how to move through a space that had been rearranged by love. The curtains stirred slightly in a breeze that had not yet arrived. Shadows hung a little longer on the floor, reluctant to dissolve.

He lit the fire, not out of cold, but ritual.

Some mornings needed warmth that didn't come from heat.

The striking of the match, the curl of the smoke, the crackle of the wood—all of it felt like prayer.

The mug sat where she last touched it—half a fingerprint still visible on the rim.

He didn't move it.

Not out of longing, but respect.

Love, to him, was not about possession, but the preservation of presence, even in absence

To erase her touch too quickly would've been like pretending it hadn't mattered. And it had. Even if only for a little while.

He made his tea in a different mug that day.

Quietly.

Deliberately.

Letting the moment be what it was, without dressing it in nostalgia or denial.

Outside, the olive tree stood in quiet vigil.

Its branches lifted slightly in the breeze, not swaying, just breathing.

He knelt beside it, the earth still soft from last night's rain. The soil held warmth beneath the surface, and he pressed his palms into it—not to plant, not to pull—just to touch something alive. He didn't pray with words. Just sat in stillness, forehead low, the way one leans into memory.

Sometimes the heart speaks in silence, and he had grown fluent in its language.

Inside, he opened his journal again.

Not to write her name.

He never had.

…But to write what remained:

—the way her laugh bent the air.

—how she said "stay" without ever saying it.

—the tie she gave him, still folded, still untouched.

—a scent in the hallway—faintly sweet, like warm amber and something unplaceable.

He didn't write out of sorrow.

He wrote to remember that something sacred had passed through him.

Even if it passed on.

Each line became a way of blessing the absence.

Not holding it hostage.

Just honoring what was.

The days that followed were not dramatic.

The church still opened its doors.

The widows still asked for help with their windows.

The garden still grew, quietly forgiving the world.

But he moved through it all slightly differently now.

Not broken.

Not bitter.

Just... changed.

He lingered longer at the edge of things—sunsets, scripture, the songs of doves overhead. He noticed the way his boots left imprints in the morning soil, how the steam from the kettle curled like incense when the light hit it just right.

He listened harder, as though the wind might carry some final note she forgot to leave behind.

Not to revive what was, but to recognize what still remained.

And in those spaces, something unexpected began to grow.

Not hope for her return.

But peace.

A deeper, rooted kind.

The kind that doesn't erase sorrow—

but blesses it.

The kind that builds a home inside loss

and plants beauty where nothing should grow.

He started humming again when he worked.

Soft tunes.

Old hymns.

Sometimes something she once sang off-key in his kitchen, laughing as she tried to remember the words.

And slowly, he began to understand:

He was not alone.

He had simply been returned to himself.
Returned gently.
Quietly.
Without bitterness.
And in the quiet ache of being left,
he found again the joy of having once been seen.

CHAPTER SEVEN:

The Sound Beneath the Applause

She arrived at the gala cloaked in satin.
Not for warmth, but spectacle.
The room shimmered with light that had no source—just reflections: chandeliers, crystal glasses, sequins, conversation. Nothing in the room glowed on its own; everything borrowed brightness. Even her.

The air was a symphony of perfumes—floral, musky, powdered—like memory trying to impress you. The music was modern, forgettable, expensive. The laughter floated above heads like confetti—cheerful and empty, landing nowhere.

Someone kissed her cheek and called her radiant.

Another whispered her name like a password into relevance.

A photographer snapped her photo and moved on before she could blink.

A journalist asked her thoughts on "presence in a distracted age." She replied with a phrase she'd said a hundred times before and believed less each time.

And for a while, she floated.

Gliding from voice to voice, hand to hand, pausing just long enough to be photographed, quoted, remembered. She accepted compliments like appetizers—small, fleeting, meant to impress rather than nourish. Everyone wore polish and conviction, but no one made room for questions without answers.

Somewhere beneath the music, something tugged.

Not regret. Not yet.

Just a quiet wondering: *What is all this built on? And why does it feel so light?*

He would have hated it here.

Not the people.

Not even the performance.

But the absence of stillness.

Here, peace was considered laziness.

Stillness, irrelevance.

Contentment, complacency.

And yet, here she was—drinking sparkling wine with people who quoted Rilke but hadn't felt anything real in years. A woman in silk asked what she *did*, not who she was. A man with clever eyes asked her opinion on digital intimacy. She answered as expected. He nodded without hearing her.

A man complimented her laugh.

Said it had texture.

She smiled politely, nodding as if that meant something.

Another praised her latest article on *"the art of grounding oneself in chaos,"* never guessing the words had been inspired by the man who once said nothing but gave her everything.

She laughed politely, then turned to refill her glass—
and paused.

She heard her own voice through a speaker in the corner—
her recorded podcast playing softly on loop. It sounded foreign now. Smoothed out. Empty of the pauses that once gave it soul.

A server passed behind her, balancing a silver tray. On it: a small votive candle in a shallow glass, flickering beneath sprigs of rosemary pressed against the wax.

The scent caught her—sudden, specific, sacred.

Not overpowering.

Just... familiar.

Her throat tightened.

She mumbled something about needing a moment, slipped through the crowd, and disappeared down the corridor—

toward the silence of the bathroom.

Later, in the bathroom, beneath a golden sconce and the lingering scent of rose water and rosemary, she stared at herself.

Painted lips.

Lashes like feathers.

Diamond pin in her hair.

It was her.

And it wasn't.

The mirror held her face gently, like a photograph someone had once believed in. The light highlighted all the parts of her she wanted the world to notice—and none of the ones she missed most.

In the mirror, she didn't see the woman who had just impressed a panel of critics.

She saw the girl who once sat cross-legged on a porch, hands wrapped around chipped ceramic, breathing in peace like it was air.

She closed her eyes and for a moment, all the sounds of the party blurred into something distant—like the hush of the countryside just before a storm. That sacred kind of hush where something old and knowing waits to be remembered.

…And in that hush, she remembered:

—the feel of his calloused hand brushing hers as they passed coffee mugs in the morning.

—the way he listened with his whole body, not just his ears.

—the soup that tasted like quiet healing.

—the sound of wind in tall grass, and the way the sky looked just before it turned to dusk.

—the tie still folded.

—the journal tucked into a drawer.

—the silence that didn't need to be filled.

Someone called her name.

She opened her eyes.

And smiled.

A perfect smile.

One made for this room.

The kind of smile you wear like armor when you realize the applause is real, but not meant for who you truly are.

And still—beneath the applause, beneath the silk, beneath the carefully chosen words—she could hear the sound of something she left behind:

A porch step creaking.

Pages turning.

Rain beginning.

A man humming an old hymn with no audience but heaven.

And the rhythm of peace
she once almost chose.

CHAPTER EIGHT:

The Grace in Staying

He rose earlier now.
Not out of sorrow, but out of rhythm.
The kind the soul keeps once it's stopped waiting to be seen.

There was no alarm, no schedule—just the internal hush that wakes a man when the world is still veiled and soft. The hour when dew forms on the windowsill, and even the birds haven't remembered their songs.

He moved slowly, but not with heaviness.
With intention.

He lit the stove with a match instead of the lighter, just to watch the flame catch from wood to warmth. He washed the dishes before the sun touched the windows. Tended the herbs with a reverence once reserved for sanctuary. Basil. Thyme. A stubborn pot of rosemary she once called "his little forest."

He prayed slowly, without agenda.
Not for answers.
Just for alignment.
Some days, he even laughed aloud at memories that once made his chest ache.
The ache had not vanished.
But it no longer ruled him.

It had been folded into the fabric of who he was—like an old hymn sewn into a quilt: unseen, but present.

One morning, a child from the congregation brought him a handful of wildflowers and a lopsided drawing of "Mr. David and the sky."

She said it shyly, the way children do when they hand over something important.

He knelt to her level and thanked her as if it were gold.

Because it was.

He pinned the drawing beside the coat hook, just under the photograph of his parents. The paper fluttered whenever the door opened, as if alive with breath. He smiled when he passed it—reminded that beauty often comes crooked, unpolished, and full of heart.

It was the first thing he saw when he left.

And the last when he returned.

He began writing again.

Not journals this time. Letters.

To no one in particular. Or maybe, to the everything that remained when a name was no longer needed.

He wrote to the wind.

To the soil.

To a future reader who may never come.

Words like water, poured out not to be preserved but to be planted. He folded the letters into a small tin box on his windowsill, each one marked only by date and a single word: *gratitude, rain, blue, enough.*

Some days he wrote about faith.

Other days about mustard seeds and unanswered prayers.

But mostly, he wrote about contentment:

"It doesn't come when all is well...

It comes when you stop needing it to be."

He found joy in those letters—not in their eloquence, but in their honesty. Each one a breadcrumb leading him deeper into the life he hadn't realized he'd already chosen.

On Sundays, he opened the drawer where the blue tie lay folded—

not to wear it, but to hold it.

He smoothed the fabric with reverent fingers,

then closed the drawer again.

Not because he hoped she'd return.

Not because he needed to be remembered.

But because it was a gift.

And gifts, even those wrapped in departure, deserve to be honored.

It was enough to touch.

Enough to remember.

Enough to remain.

The porch, once shared, became his again.

Not lonelier.

Just fuller in its silence.

The rocking chair creaked only when he moved it. The cup beside him held no second pair of fingerprints. But the absence did not accuse—it blessed.

The wind returned to its whispering.

The doves resumed their songs.

The bell above the church door rang every morning, and he heard it like a psalm that belonged to no one and everyone.

And when the olive tree dropped a few more leaves, he swept them slowly—

Not to tidy.
But to remember:
Everything falls.
Everything returns.
Everything, in time,
finds its way back to grace.

The Leaving

"*You were the melody I never stopped humming, even when the world around me fell quiet.*" — *From the Journal*

CHAPTER NINE:

The Stranger by the Well

The well hadn't run dry.
But the rope had frayed.
He noticed it one morning while drawing water, the fibers worn and splintering like tired promises. It caught in his hand—a small sting, the kind that wakes a man gently, like truth whispered before dawn. He made a mental note to repair it—though truthfully, he wasn't sure how. It was the kind of task he usually enjoyed, but lately, his hands moved slower. Not in pain—just time.

The kind of slowness that comes when your body and your soul agree that rushing has nothing left to offer.

That's when he saw her.

A woman, maybe in her early forties, walking the path like she'd done it before, though he'd never seen her face. She wasn't from the town. Her boots weren't dusty. Her coat still carried the creases of the city. But her eyes—her eyes were tired in the way that people are when they've seen too much and rested too little.

She paused when she reached the gate.

Looked at the porch, then the tree, then him.

"Am I trespassing?" she asked.

He shook his head.

"Not unless you're planning to steal the sky."

She smiled at that.

The kind of smile that comes not from humor—but from recognition.

From hearing something your soul already knew, spoken aloud by a stranger.

She asked for water.

He offered a seat.

And together, they sat beneath the olive tree, drinking in more than silence. The branches arched over them like an old cathedral, sunlight dappling the ground in patches that shifted as they spoke.

She said her name was Miriam.

Didn't give a last name.

Didn't need one.

She sat like someone who didn't know how tired she was until she stopped moving.

He didn't ask why she came.

People arrive when they're meant to, and often for reasons they themselves don't yet know.

But she talked.

A little.

Said she'd been driving, aimless, weary. Said she had missed her exit twice on purpose. Said she saw the tree and felt… called to it.

"Like something old lives here," she said.

He nodded.

"Something does."

They spoke of small things—soil and seeds, wind and weariness.

She asked about the tie.

He didn't lie.

Just said, "It was a gift."

She didn't press.

Instead, she told him about the noise.

How cities grow louder, not with sound, but with need.

How people forget themselves in places like that.

How kindness begins to feel like a foreign language spoken only by the lonely.

She said her apartment had floor-to-ceiling windows but no view that ever calmed her

That even the sky there felt artificial.

He didn't offer advice.

He simply listened.

And when she finished,

he said softly:

"Stillness isn't where you go.

It's what you carry when you leave."

She didn't reply.

But something in her shoulders softened—

as though some invisible bag had been set down,

and she hadn't realized how long she'd been carrying it.

There was a quiet, contemplative pause.

Then she said, almost to herself, "Funny... I thought I was coming here to forget something."

She glanced at the olive tree again. "But maybe I needed to remember something instead."

He didn't answer. Just let the silence stretch—like a field left open for planting.

Before she left, she looked at the tree again.

It shimmered slightly in the late morning light, its bark etched with quiet resilience.

"You take good care of it," she said.

"It takes care of me," he replied.

She stepped up onto the porch, then turned back.

There was something grateful in her eyes.

Not for what had been said, but for what hadn't.

She placed a folded note on the bench.

"You don't need to open it now."

Then she walked away.

Not hurried.

Not heavy.

Just… changed.

As she disappeared down the road, he watched her with the kind of gaze reserved for rare things—not because they are yours, but because they passed through and left you better.

Some visitors, he had learned, are not just passing strangers… but quiet confirmations.

Inside, he unfolded the note hours later.

Her handwriting was careful, as though every word had been chosen like a stone for a sacred path.

"Thank you for your silence.

In it, I heard everything I'd forgotten I needed to remember."

He placed the note beside the others he never re-read but never threw away.

Notes from visitors, from seekers, from lives that had passed through his without warning and left something behind.

Not souvenirs.

But seeds.

And as dusk folded into the room, he returned to the well.

The rope still frayed.
But the water—
clear as grace—
waited patiently below.

CHAPTER TEN:

The Cost of Climbing

The penthouse had a view.

Of everything, and nothing.

Glass stretched from floor to ceiling, offering the skyline like a trophy—wrapped in fog and golden hues and all the things she used to chase. Skyscrapers blinked like weary stars, and the streets below hummed with lives she could no longer hear clearly. From this high up, the people looked like ants.

Even the laughter of the city sounded far away.

Contained. Distant.

Muted, like a memory behind glass.

She stood barefoot on the marble floor, silk robe wrapped tightly around her, espresso untouched on the tray beside her. The cup had been poured an hour ago, but she had forgotten to drink it. Or maybe she had intended not to.

The man she'd married—briefly—was gone now.

Not dead. Just… exited.

Like most things in her life.

Quietly. Politely. Without apology.

She hadn't fought it.

She hadn't even cried.

There had been no betrayal. No broken vows.

Just… a dissolving.

Like salt into water.

She pressed her palm to the window. It was cold despite the heat inside, a thin layer of glass separating her from the chaos she once believed she belonged to. The world looked cinematic from here—curated, distant, beautiful in that dispassionate way success often is.

There were invitations piled on the kitchen counter—galas, openings, luncheons with women who spoke in compliments and critiques without changing tone.

She had mastered their dialect.

She could nod with sincerity while silently disagreeing.

She knew how to disappear in a conversation without ever leaving the room.

But she hadn't learned their joy.

Or maybe they hadn't, either.

She walked past the mirror in the hallway, barely glancing.

She already knew what she'd see:

polish, poise, perfection.

Not warmth.

Not wonder.

The kind of beauty that asks for applause but never for understanding.

She had built herself a cathedral of glass—tall, gleaming, echoing.

Her life had grown taller. Shinier.

But never wider.

And she felt it now—how narrow it had all become.

Later that night, she sat in the corner of the rooftop lounge, alone, watching couples spin across the floor. The music was elegant. Safe. Measured.

The kind you nod to, not dance with.

She nursed a drink she didn't care for. Her dress shimmered in the low light. Strangers smiled at her, paused, moved on. Everyone knew her name.

No one knew her.

She remembered when music used to make her want to close her eyes.

She remembered him.

Not his face, exactly.

But the stillness he carried.

The way he looked at the world as though it were already enough.

The way he looked at her as though she were too.

He never tried to impress her.

Never needed to.

He made silence feel like a place, not an absence.

She sipped her drink.

Smiled at a stranger.

Said something clever.

But somewhere, beneath the practiced laugh, she heard it—that voice.

Not his.

Hers.

The one that used to hum old songs in kitchens that smelled like tomatoes and thyme.

The one that read poetry aloud while barefoot.

The one that once cried into folded hands and didn't need to explain why.

The one that believed in small things.

In quiet men.

In kindness that didn't ask for attention.
She hadn't heard that voice in years.
And suddenly, she missed her.
The woman she used to be.
She excused herself early.
No one questioned her.
No one followed.
The elevator chimed softly as she stepped inside.
She didn't press the button right away.
Just stared at her reflection in the mirrored paneling.
So composed.
So polished.
And somehow, it felt... hollow.
As though everything she had climbed for had left her
breathless at the top
and still
alone.

CHAPTER ELEVEN:

A Life with Edges

She hadn't planned on reading the interview.
She barely remembered subscribing to the magazine.
But there it was—in the latest issue of *Urban Faith & Culture*, tucked between an essay on reinvention and a glossy piece on moral branding, each page thick with language that sounded important but rarely said anything worth keeping.

The headline read:

"Stillness Speaks: A Conversation with the Stranger Who Chose the Backroads."

She nearly flipped past it.
The photograph didn't catch her eye.
The name of the interviewer rang no bells.
But the subtitle did:

"On simplicity, reverence, and why love doesn't always stay."

That line lodged itself in her chest.
Not painful.
But sharp.
She began reading without meaning to.

Skimming at first.
Then slowing.
Then stopping.

"Sometimes,"

the woman being interviewed said,

"the holiest people are the ones you almost didn't notice.
The ones who greet you with silence and send you away with clarity."

Another line:

"We think wisdom comes from answers, but I've found it more often
in pauses. In people who walk slowly, love quietly, and keep no
record of who owes them what."

And then, this:

"He never preached. He didn't have to. He just lived. And being
near that kind of peace—it makes you question the noise you've
called purpose."

Her hand trembled.
She told herself it was the coffee.
Too strong.
Too cold.
She closed the magazine.
But the words didn't close with it.
The evening gala was black-tie.

She wore red.

Not crimson. Not wine.

Red.

Not because she wanted to stand out.

But because she was tired of disappearing into gracefulness.

The dress was structured, perfect. The kind stylists called "intentional." But she felt like a guest in her own skin. Like she'd been dressed for someone else's story.

Men toasted her name.

Women praised her latest column on *"strategic solitude."*

She laughed.

Nodded.

Danced when expected.

But the echo of the stranger's words trailed her like perfume she hadn't meant to wear. Something subtle and sacred clung to her.

The words had struck a match in a room she had worked years to keep dim.

She tried to shake it off.

Told herself she had chosen wisely.

After all:

—she was respected.

—she was comfortable.

—she was visible.

But comfort, she was learning, had corners.

Corners that pinched at night.

Corners that grew darker the longer you sat in them.

Corners that whispered things mirrors would never say.

And visibility, she realized, was not the same as being seen.

Later that night, she opened the drawer beneath her nightstand.

Not looking for anything.

Just restless.

Inside, beneath old notes and receipts and a boarding pass to Madrid she never used, lay a photograph.

Not of him.

But of the olive tree.

She had taken it one autumn afternoon, not knowing why.

The angle was crooked.

The light uneven.

Leaves caught mid-motion.

And there, near the edge, barely visible—

a shadow.

A hand.

His hand.

She had forgotten she even kept it.

Now, she stared.

She remembered the way the tree felt when she leaned against it—warm, real, rooted.

She remembered the bench.

The silence.

The peace she mistook for smallness.

He never once asked her to stay.

Never made her choose.

He simply offered his world like a steady bench beneath a tree—

and trusted her to know the worth of rest.

She once thought that made him weak.

Now she wondered if it made him holy.

She climbed into bed.

The sheets were cool.

The city buzzed below her, vibrant and full.

But inside, it was still.

Sleep did not come.

Instead, the silence did—

dense, honest, sacred.

The kind she used to call boring.

The kind he carried like an inheritance.

And in that silence, a question rose she could no longer quiet:

"What if the life I built is beautiful...

but not mine?"

CHAPTER TWELVE:

The Letter She Never Sent

It was a Tuesday.

Or maybe a Thursday.

One of those days that feels like the pause between footsteps—unremarkable on the outside, but holding its breath beneath the surface.

The kind of day that doesn't announce anything, but changes everything.

Rain tapped gently against the tall hotel windows like a clock trying to remind her of something she didn't want to remember.

Not the date.

Not the time.

Something older. Closer to the bone.

The kind of memory that speaks in feeling before it forms into thought.

The room was too quiet.

Too clean.

Not clean like tidy.

Clean like hollow.

Like someone had wiped away every fingerprint but forgot to remove the echo.

She sat at the edge of the bed in a silk blouse and heels she hadn't yet taken off.

Her legs were crossed, but not comfortably.

Her hair was still pinned. Her lipstick faded slightly at the corners. She looked like someone who had just returned from a success she didn't believe in.

The kind of victory that only counts when you say it aloud too many times.

Her reflection wavered in the mirror across the room. Blurry.

Not from movement, but from the ache in the air.

Humidity. Or maybe memory.

Something invisible that pressed against the chest like longing with no clear origin.

Somewhere below, a jazz trio played for strangers laughing over olives and martinis and the price of things.

She envied their laughter.

Not its ease, but its ignorance.

She reached for her phone.

Scrolled.

Paused.

Set it down again.

Then, without knowing exactly why, she opened the drawer in the nightstand.

Not out of curiosity.

Out of ache.

Inside: hotel stationery—crisp, faintly perfumed with something floral.

The kind of scent meant to evoke comfort, but only reminded her of rooms that didn't belong to anyone.

She picked up the pen.

Paused.

Put it down.
Picked it up again.

Dear—

She stopped. Crossed it out.

To the one who still lingers.

Too poetic. Too careful.
She scratched it out again.
And then,
without ceremony,
without guarding herself,
she began to write.
Not like a woman composing a letter.
But like a soul finally laying down the weight it could no longer
carry.

I don't know why I'm writing this.
Maybe because silence has grown heavy.
Maybe because your name still hums like a hymn beneath the noise of
this new life.
Or maybe because there's something about rain in a strange city that
makes people tell the truth.
I saw you again last night.
Not really—you weren't there.
But I saw someone with your eyes.
Not their color. Not their shape.
But their gentleness.

The kind that doesn't look through you but into you.
And I realized how rare that is.

    I used to think you wanted too little out of life.
That your quiet was a kind of resignation.
But I was wrong.
You wanted the kind of things that couldn't be bought.
And I... I wanted to want those things too.
I just didn't know how.

    You scared me, in a way.
Not because you were dangerous.
But because you were steady.
Because you saw me when I didn't even know I was lost.
And I didn't know how to stand still back then.
Still don't. Most days.

    But tonight I wanted to write this.
Not to ask for anything.
Not to explain.
Just to say...

    You mattered.
More than I let on.
More than I probably understood.

She stared at the words.
Then added:

    I wanted to choose you.
    And part of me still wonders if I would have found myself anyway—
if I had stayed.
Or maybe...
Maybe you were the home I left looking for.

I was wrong.
I thought I knew what I wanted.
But I didn't.
I don't even know how to finish this without—

Her hand stopped.

The pen hovered.

She blinked.

Once.

Twice.

Then set the pen down gently,
as if waking someone.

She folded the letter slowly, precisely—like one might fold a flag or a memory too fragile to crumple.

She didn't address it.

Didn't stamp it.

Didn't even place it in an envelope.

Instead, she reached for the book on the nightstand—

The Presence of Knowing—

and tucked the letter between *"As I Walked Along the Garden Path"* and *"The Quiet After the Storm."*

She rested her hand on the closed cover.

Held it there longer than needed.

Not because she was unsure.

But because, somehow, in that moment of stillness...

She almost felt held.

And there it stayed.

Unsent.

Unread.

Unforgotten.

CHAPTER THIRTEEN:

The Measure of a Man

He didn't own a pulpit.
Never raised his voice from behind a lectern.
But faith lived in him the way breath lived in lungs—quiet, constant, unseen until the moment it was needed most.

He spoke to God like someone who knew silence well enough to listen back.

Not the silence of emptiness.

The silence of knowing you are not alone, even when you are the only one in the room.

He didn't wear crosses.

Didn't quote verses to win arguments.

Didn't post about belief or battle for doctrine.

He simply lived it.

Beneath the surface.

In the way he mended what was torn, noticed what was missing, forgave what others discarded.

In the mornings, before the town stirred, he'd sit on his porch with a chipped mug and a worn Bible—its cover faded, pages marked by weather and oil from his fingers. He didn't read it to feel holy.

He read it to feel held.

He underlined not the promises, but the questions.

The ones whispered in Psalms and shadowed in the Gospels.

He traced the margins with his thumb, not as a scholar but as a pilgrim.

One morning, he scribbled a prayer in the margin:

"I'm not asking for riches.

I'm asking to remain good even when the world forgets what good looks like."

That morning, the light fell softly across the page, like a benediction.

The church didn't always understand him.

He wasn't flashy enough. Didn't dress the part. Never sought the stage or the handshake or the nod of approval. He didn't join committees or submit ideas. He simply showed up.

But the elders knew his name.

Not because he campaigned for it—
but because he carried weight.

The kind of weight that steadied a room.

The kind that didn't shift with trends or titles.

He helped repair the steps when the wood began to rot.

Replaced bulbs in the sanctuary without being asked.

Carried hymnals for the woman with arthritic hands.

Once, when the new preacher stumbled on his first sermon, voice cracking under the weight of nervousness, it was this man who clapped first.

Just once.

Just enough.

And somehow, it steadied the whole room.

No one forgot that.

He kept a stack of handwritten prayers in a tin box beside his bed.

Not requests.

Just names.

People he had met.

People who never knew he prayed for them.

Neighbors.

A cashier who looked weary.

A man from the bus station with a limp and no luggage.

The child from down the road who loved butterflies but feared thunder.

And her.

Always her.

He never prayed for her to return.

Only for her well-being.

Her clarity.

Her joy.

"Lord, teach me how to love without agenda.
Let me be peace to those who pass through—
even if they never stay."

Some nights, he wrestled with doubt.

He never denied it.

Never pretended the path was without shadows.

He had asked God once,

"Why does the world chase after noise,
when You whisper?"

But no answer came that night.

Only a breeze through the open window.
Only stillness.

And somehow, that was enough.

Because he knew—

not all answers come as sentences.

Some come as presence.

He didn't need to be right.

He only needed to remain faithful.

And so, when people spoke of saints, they thought of altars
and miracles.

But if they had looked closer—
they would've seen him.

Not shining.

Not shouting.

Just sweeping the church steps at dawn.

Measuring a man not by his sermons—
but by the shadows he gently turned into light.

He didn't need applause.

But sometimes, even the quietest lives are noticed—
by those who've lived long enough to understand,
and by those young enough to still be watching.

CHAPTER FOURTEEN:
The Elders Visit

The knock came just before sunset.

Three soft raps—no urgency, no insistence.
Just the kind of knock that knew it could wait.

He rose slowly from his chair, setting aside the mug he never quite emptied and the book he never quite finished. His joints protested mildly, but he welcomed the ache—it was proof he was still here.

Outside, the day was settling into itself—
the golden hour that always made the olive tree cast longer shadows,
like it was stretching,
reaching backward before letting go.

At the door stood Brother Ellison—one of the elders from the church.

Wide-brimmed hat, leather-bound Bible under one arm,
and a brown sack tucked under the other.

"Evenin'," the elder said with a nod.
"Evenin'," he replied.

No more was needed.

He stepped aside.

They sat on the porch without fanfare.

Just two men and a sky slowly folding itself into twilight.

The man offered sweet tea; the elder declined.

"Doctor says I've had too many sweet things for one life."

He chuckled. "You've had more bitter things than most, too."

The elder shrugged. "Balance."

They fell into an easy hush—the kind forged by years of shared service and mutual respect. No filling of space, no rush to speak.

The breeze stirred gently through the olive tree.

It wasn't performing.

Just being.

After a while, the elder reached into the sack and pulled out a loaf of bread—still warm.

"Made by Sister Lydia," he said. "She bakes when she worries. You must be heavy on her heart."

The man took it with both hands, reverently.

"Tell her thank you. I'm not much for fuss, but I'll receive what's given."

They both chuckled softly at that—knowing well that sometimes bread is more than bread. Sometimes it's a prayer with a crust.

They spoke a little.

Of gardens. Of rain. Of the new hymnbook the choir didn't like.

Of how the pews creaked in different places now that Brother Harris had moved up front.

Then the elder turned to him—not all at once, just enough to see him clearly.

"You know, some folks in town don't see you."

He nodded.

Not bitterly.

Just… knowingly.

"But some of us do."

The man didn't speak. Just waited.

"You've never asked for anything.

Never asked to be called leader or saint.

You just… serve."

The elder's voice quieted.

"And I've come to think—
maybe you've preached more sermons with your silence
than any of us with our mouths."

That caught him.

Not pride.

Not flattery.

But something deeper.

Like a stone settling at the bottom of a well.

He smiled, humble and steady.

"I just try to leave the world a little softer than I found it."

Brother Ellison nodded slowly.

"That's the kind of softness the world doesn't wear down.

It remembers."

He stood and reached into his coat, pulling out a folded paper.
"No rush, but we're updating the elders' board. Thought you
ought to know there's an open seat."

The man looked at the paper but didn't reach for it.

"I'm no preacher," he said softly.

"We've got enough preachers," the elder replied.

"What we need is presence."

He didn't answer.

Just looked out at the fading light, the long stretch of land,
the olive tree holding its own shape against the dusk.

Brother Ellison tipped his hat.

"I reckon you've already done more leading than most of us.

But if not—keep going.

Some of us are following, even if we don't say it."

And with that, he stepped off the porch and disappeared down the path.

The man sat there a little longer.

The bread still warm in his hands.

The sun bowing behind the hills.

And something inside him loosening—

not because it needed recognition,

but because it had received witness.

And sometimes, that was all the soul needed to keep going.

The porch remained quiet after the elder left.

But something had shifted—gently, almost imperceptibly.

As if legacy had spoken, and the silence now hummed with its echo.

And in that stillness, another kind of visitor came—

not with words, but with wonder.

CHAPTER FIFTEEN:

The Boy and the Garden

He noticed the boy on a Thursday.
Small. Thin. Always walking with his head down,
like he didn't want to be noticed
and had been anyway, too many times.

His backpack was torn at one corner.
One shoelace was knotted in a hurry.
The sleeves of his jacket reached past his wrists like they were hiding him.

The boy passed his garden gate every morning on the way to school and again in the afternoon—always alone, always silent.

At first, he didn't say anything.
Just nodded.
A small gesture.
An invitation without pressure.

The boy never nodded back.
Not at first.

But one afternoon, when the boy stopped and stared too long at the tomato vines,
he asked,
"You hungry?"

The boy didn't answer.
He just shrugged.

A shrug that said more than it withheld.

So the man picked the ripest tomato, brushed it clean, cut it open with a pocketknife, sprinkled a little salt from a paper packet he kept in his back pocket, and handed it over.

The boy took it.

A little too quickly.

He bit into it like he didn't trust it would still be there in the next breath.

He ate in silence.

Didn't say thank you.

Didn't need to.

The next day, the boy came back.

Didn't speak.

Just stood at the gate.

So the man handed him a trowel and pointed toward a row of empty soil.

"That's yours," he said. "If you want it."

The boy didn't smile.

But he stepped forward.

That was enough.

Over the weeks, the boy returned.

Same time each afternoon.

Still quiet. Still cautious.

But his hands grew steadier.

His eyes stayed longer.

He learned how to plant, how to weed, how to trim without harming the stems. He learned patience, and how the soil doesn't respond to shouting—only to stillness.

The man never asked about his home life.

He didn't need to.

Some stories are told in what someone doesn't say—
in the way they flinch at loud voices,
or never look up when praised.

Instead, the man gave the boy what the soil gave him:
Space.
Warmth.
Time.

And for the first time,
the boy grew.

One day, the boy asked,
"Why do you do all this?"

The man wiped his hands on his jeans and looked at the garden.
Sunlight filtered through the olive tree, soft as prayer.

"For the same reason you come back," he said.

The boy frowned. "And what's that?"

He smiled.
"Because some things need tending."

The boy didn't respond—
not with words.

But the next day, he arrived earlier.
Worked quieter.
Listened more.
He learned how to plant, how to weed,
how to wait.

Not because someone taught him—
but because someone made room for him to learn.
And his hands grew steadier with each passing day.

The man never asked why he now came earlier each morning.

He simply handed him the trowel and let the soil teach him
what words could not.

There were no lectures. No life lessons.
Only the rhythm of care:
pulling weeds, watering roots,
and letting things grow at their own pace.

One afternoon, the boy placed a small stone at the edge of
the row—
not as a marker, but as a gesture.
A thank-you.
A prayer.

The man didn't ask what it meant.
He just nodded.

As the boy pressed the last seed into the ground,
the man watched silently,
knowing that some things take root
not because they are told to,
but because they are given time.

And when summer waned
and the boy no longer came,
the man didn't wonder where he'd gone.

Life pulls people different ways.
The garden still bloomed.
The soil still offered its quiet miracles.
And the man waited without waiting.

Because love, once planted,
has its own way of returning.

The Rooting

"They that sow in tears shall reap in joy." — Psalm 126:5

CHAPTER SIXTEEN:

Sanctuary and Reflection

The chapel was empty.
Not abandoned—just quiet in the way sacred places are when no one's watching.
Like it had exhaled after years of holding breath.
Like it knew the difference between being filled and being full.

She hadn't stepped inside a church in years.

Not since ambition replaced prayer
and her Sunday mornings became brunches, not benedictions.

Not since faith became something ornamental—kept at a distance, spoken of only when poetic.

But something about this small stone chapel called to her.

Maybe it was the ivy coiled around its bell tower,
or the way the doors didn't creak when they opened—
just whispered.

It smelled faintly of wax and cedar.

Of paper Bibles with frayed ribbons.

Of things too old to fake their age and too sacred to modernize.

She didn't sit in the front.

Or the back.

She chose the middle.

Because she wasn't seeking distance or spotlight.

Only honesty.

The stained glass cast slow-moving rainbows across the pews.

They reminded her of his windows—
the way light filtered through them in the morning, catching on dust and hope alike.

He once told her,
"Light doesn't discriminate.
It just reveals."

She remembered how he used to pause, coffee in hand,
just to admire the way morning looked when it touched ordinary things.

The way he called that light holy—
not because it came from heaven,
but because it touched the mundane without hesitation.

She never understood it then.

Now she ached for it.

A woman hummed softly in the back room—
some old hymn she couldn't name.

The notes drifted like warm steam,
carrying with them a hush that softened everything it touched.

The kind of song that didn't require harmony.

Just sincerity.

She closed her eyes, letting the melody hold her like a story she once knew by heart.

And then, without warning, the tears came.

Not loud.

Not theatrical.

Just soft drops falling down a face
that had too often smiled out of necessity.

She didn't cry for him.

Not exactly.

She cried for the version of herself that once knew how to kneel.

She didn't know what she was asking for.

Forgiveness?

Maybe.

Clarity?

Possibly.

But mostly,

she wanted to be seen again.

Not as someone's keynote speaker.

Not as a well-dressed ideal.

Not as an article, a portfolio, a brand.

Just…

as the girl who once sat under an olive tree and felt safe.

After a while, she wandered into the side room where prayer candles flickered.

Each flame a silent whisper,

each glass cup holding someone's ache.

She lit one without speaking.

No grand prayer.

Just presence.

Watched the flame rise, then steady—

the way she used to steady herself against his silence.

She sat for a while in the hush, her hands clasped, not in piety but in stillness.

Not asking.

Just listening.

Just remembering what it felt like to have nothing to prove.

As she turned to leave, she caught her reflection in the polished glass of the vestibule door.

And for a moment, she didn't recognize herself.

Not because she looked older.

Or tired.

But because—beneath the tailored coat, the sculpted hair, the practiced poise—
she saw something she had forgotten:

The woman he once saw
before she ever knew how to be seen.

And in that glance,
she forgave herself—
a little.

Outside, the sky had softened.

The light was thinning in that golden way it does when the day is not yet over, but has started to let go.

As she stepped outside,
the wind lifted a leaf into her path.

Amber, speckled, veined like a map of memory.

She bent, picked it up, and smiled—
not because it meant something grand.

But because it reminded her of stillness.

And stillness,
she was learning,
is often the doorway back to truth.

CHAPTER SEVENTEEN:

When the Wind Changes

It began with the kettle.
He had filled it, placed it over the flame, and waited—as he always did—for the water to sing.
But this time, he noticed the quiet before the steam.
A pause. A hush.

The kind that wraps around you without warning, like a shawl placed gently on your shoulders.

And in that hush,
he felt something.

Not sorrow.

Not joy.

Just... presence.

Like someone had spoken his name on the other side of the world,
and the echo had found its way home.

He didn't rush the moment.

Didn't chase it.

Just let it be—like you do with wind chimes on a still day, when the air stirs just enough to whisper.

The morning light was softer than usual, laying gold across the windowsill like the memory of warmth.

The birds sang differently.

Not louder, but deeper—like they weren't just filling the silence,
but answering it.

Even the shadows stretched differently, like they remembered something they weren't supposed to forget.

He sat on the porch with his notebook open but unwritten.

A pencil tucked behind his ear.

The kind of stillness that didn't need to be productive.

There were no words yet.

Only breath.

Only presence.

And the strange, beautiful ache of something unspoken being heard.

He thought of her.

Not vividly.

Not with longing.

Just a name whispered through memory, like a breeze through the branches of the olive tree.

Her laugh as it once was—carefree, unexpected, like a skipped stone.

Her gaze, just before it turned away.

Her hands, folding a letter she never sent.

The blue tie she gave him,
still hanging neatly where he left it.

He closed his eyes.

And in that quiet place, he prayed.

Not for reunion.

Not even for closure.

But for softening.

That whatever hard shell she'd learned to wear,

might crack just enough
for the light to touch her again.

Later that day, he walked the length of the garden, now overrun with wild mint and thyme.

It had become unruly in the most sacred way—
not neglected, but freed.

He didn't tame it.

He let it grow.

Some things are more beautiful
when left slightly undone.

The bees hummed a low praise song between blossoms.

The breeze carried the scent of something he couldn't quite name, but knew he'd once loved.

He passed the olive tree, now heavy with silence and years, and paused beneath its reach.

His hand grazed the bark.

A small act.

A prayer without words.

He didn't speak aloud.

But in his chest, there was this:

"I felt her today."

He didn't need confirmation.

Some truths don't require proof.

They just arrive, and settle, and stay.

That evening, as the sun folded itself into the horizon like a benediction,
he lit a single candle and placed it by the window.

Not as a beacon.

Not as a call.

But as a welcome.

For whatever might return.
Or whoever.
He watched the flame flicker.
Watched the room soften under its glow.
And with a quiet breath, he whispered:
"Let it be enough."

CHAPTER EIGHTEEN:

The Market

It began with the kettle.
He hadn't planned to see her that day.
He was only there for tomatoes.

The small Saturday market on the outskirts of town buzzed with its usual quiet charm—
crates of sun-warmed produce, tables draped in faded cloth, the scent of rosemary and dust and conversation.

It was the kind of place people came not just to buy,
but to remember what it felt like to slow down.

Mothers bartered over peaches.
A man in overalls played an old fiddle near the edge of the stalls.

Children chased one another between booths, giggling like the world was still wide and full of wonder.

He moved through it all with the ease of someone who belonged,
not because he demanded space—
but because he never tried to take more than he needed.

She had wandered in by accident.
Or maybe on purpose.
She would never say.

She was with friends—laughing a little too loudly,
her sunglasses perched like armor across her face.

A linen scarf looped loosely at her neck.

An iced coffee in one hand, her phone in the other.

The kind of casual grace that took hours to perfect.

He spotted her before she saw him—
halfway between the honey stall and the old woman selling fresh basil out of jelly jars.

She looked… out of place.

Not in the way city folk sometimes do—
overdressed for simplicity,
but in the way someone looks when their life has been speaking in one dialect
and suddenly hears another.

He was at the tomato stand,
weighing heirlooms in his palms like small promises.

The farmer behind the booth greeted him by name,
handed him a bag without asking.

"You always pick the ugliest ones," the farmer chuckled.

"They have the most flavor," he replied, smiling, turning one over in his hand like a memory.

That's when she saw him.

Their eyes met—briefly, but wholly.

The kind of glance that carries a hundred unspoken pages in a single beat.

Not accusatory. Not awkward.

Just honest.

"Hello," she said, almost startled by her own voice.

"Morning," he answered, tucking the tomatoes into a canvas sack.

"Didn't expect to see you here."

"I didn't expect to be here," she said honestly.

There was a pause.

Not awkward.

Just unhurried.

The air between them filled with the scent of earth and possibility.

She looked down at the tomatoes, wrinkled and uneven in color.

"You're really buying these?"

He held one up between them, its red streaked with yellow like a sunset that had forgotten to end.

"They're the best kind," he said. "Not pretty. But honest."

She smirked, a little unsure.

"You always did have a fondness for strange things."

He didn't respond right away.

Just held her gaze for a breath too long.

"I like things that grow in crooked places," he said quietly.

"They're the ones that survive."

She looked away.

A friend called her name from across the lot—

something about wine samples and a gallery event that evening.

She gave a small, polite nod and turned to go,

but then paused.

"You ever tire of all this?" she asked.

"Of small towns and ugly tomatoes and people who know your name?"

He considered the question.

Not defensively. Not romantically.

Just truly.

Then smiled.

"No. But I've learned that not everyone's built for staying."

81

She opened her mouth to say something,
but the words didn't arrive in time.

So she just nodded.

And left.

He watched her disappear into the crowd,
her presence folding back into the noise
like a stone into a river—
visible only for a moment
before the surface smoothed.

But he kept the tomato she had stared at.

Didn't put it in the bag.

Just held it, thoughtfully, like you do with things that almost
mattered more.

Later that evening,
he sliced it thin,
sprinkled it with sea salt,
and ate it with an old spoon.

No wine. No company.

Just the taste of something imperfect and real.

It was the last tomato of the season.

And somehow,
it tasted like goodbye.

CHAPTER NINETEEN:

The Tie That Remained

The day had started like most others—quiet, unspectacular. The kettle had whistled before sunrise.

The porch creaked under his weight in all the usual places.

The birds had sung as they always did—without audience or expectation.

The olive tree cast long shadows over the worn wooden floor as morning poured gently through the window, staining the room gold in that soft, forgiving way that light sometimes does when it forgets to be urgent.

He moved slowly now.

Not out of pain.

But out of reverence.

Everything felt sacred these days.

Even folding laundry.

Especially folding laundry.

There was something holy in the rhythm—shirts smoothed, socks matched, sleeves aligned like prayer hands.

And that's when he saw it.

Tucked in the back of the drawer, wrapped in an old linen handkerchief with a hand-stitched border, lay the tie.

The one she'd given him all those years ago.

It hadn't been fancy.

Just a simple navy pattern with faint stitched lines—elegant, understated, not quite him.

A little too polished for his wardrobe, a little too modern for his rhythm.

But he had kept it.

Not because it matched anything.

Not because it was useful.

But because it came from her.

He unfolded the handkerchief with the same care one might give to a delicate relic, as if the memory stitched into the fabric might crumble if handled too quickly.

He lifted the tie, the fabric softer now with age, the scent of lavender long faded.

The kind of scent you don't notice until it's gone, and then you miss it without understanding why.

He didn't hold it to his cheek.

Didn't clutch it to his chest.

He wasn't the sort to dramatize small things.

Instead, he simply smoothed the length of it with his palm, thumb pressing gently into the stitching, as though reading a letter written without ink.

He set it gently across the back of the chair.

He'd wear it soon.

He didn't know when.

But he would.

Not for a service.

Not for a statement.

Just because she gave it.

And that was enough.

It was not an heirloom.

It was not even his favorite.

But it had been offered in a moment of closeness—
a shared warmth that didn't last, but mattered.

And sometimes,
what remains is not the grand gesture,
but the small offering that time forgets to take.

He sat for a while after that.

Hands folded in his lap.

The tie beside him like a quiet witness.

He thought of the way she handed it to him back then—
awkwardly, as if unsure whether it was the right thing.

He had said thank you.

She had smiled, but quickly.

And then changed the subject.

It hadn't seemed meaningful.

Not in the moment.

But now—
now that his days were slow and the world quieter—
now that her shadow no longer stretched across his porch or her
laugh no longer echoed in his kitchen—
it was one of the few things left
that still carried her.

He didn't long for her.

Not anymore.

But he honored what had passed through.

The tie remained on the chair all that day.

He didn't move it.

Didn't wear it.

Just let it be.

Like a keepsake of grace.

Like a ribbon tied between memory and mercy.
Later that night, before bed,
he folded it again.
Carefully.
Lovingly.
Placed it back in the drawer.
Didn't close it all the way.
Let it breathe.
Because love, even the kind that doesn't stay,
sometimes needs a little air.

The Returning

"I have learned that love is not proven by how it ends, but by how it endures when no one's watching." — From the Journal

CHAPTER TWENTY:

The Mirror

It hung in the hallway, opposite the bedroom door—oval, tarnished at the edges, its frame carved with vines that time had softened until they looked more like rivers than leaves.

He passed it every day.

Barely noticed it anymore.

But tonight,

he paused.

Not out of vanity.

Not even out of nostalgia.

But because the light had caught it differently—

moonlight, fractured through the old curtains, casting a pale shimmer across the glass like breath upon a window.

The house was quiet.

The kind of quiet that settles after decades—after prayers, after music, after footsteps have memorized the floorboards.

Even the olive tree outside had stilled.

And in that stillness,

he looked at himself.

Not long.

Just long enough to wonder.

His beard had grown in full—gray now, though he didn't mind.

It suited him.

Like stone suits a path, or twilight suits the sky.

His hands were calloused, gentle.

One knuckle slightly crooked from an old injury never treated.

His shoulders had softened, not from weakness,
but from years of carrying things that couldn't be seen.

But it was his eyes he studied.

Still the same shade of wondering blue.

Not piercing.

Not vivid.

Just... honest.

There was a time she had said they looked like hope.

Then later, like home.

Then, eventually—
like nothing at all.

He didn't hold it against her.

Truth has seasons too.

And not all seasons are meant to stay green.

He reached up and straightened his tie.

The same one she had given him years ago—
blue with a subtle silver thread running through it like the glint of something barely remembered.

He never wore it out.

Only here, at night.

Before sleep.

Before prayer.

It wasn't ritual.

It was remembrance.

Somehow, it helped him feel less alone.

He looked into the mirror once more.

"What did she see?" he whispered.

Not bitter.

Not angry.

Just curious.

Like someone tracing the outline of a question they never asked aloud.

"What didn't she?"

The mirror gave no answers.

Only reflection.

Only the soft echo of being seen by something that would never speak.

But sometimes—
that's enough.

He reached for the photo tucked just behind the frame.

Not a portrait.

Just a moment.

A town picnic.

Children chasing ribbons.

People laughing.

And in the background—
there she was.

Head tilted back in laughter.

Eyes alight with something unreachable.

Not looking at him.

Not even near him.

But present.

He hadn't taken the photo.

Someone else had.

But he had kept it.

Not to cling—
only to remember
that once,
joy had bloomed near him.
     And that was enough.
     He placed the photo back gently,
the edge just peeking from the frame.
     Then turned away.
     From the mirror.
     From the questions.
     Some things, he had learned,
are better left to silence.
     Like echoes.
     Or love that never had the chance to answer.
     Or a name spoken only once in prayer,
then released.
     The hallway grew dim as the moon passed behind a cloud.
     His footsteps softened into the floor.
     And the mirror—
old, steady, patient—
remained behind him,
holding the image of a man
who never demanded to be seen,
but had chosen to see anyway.

CHAPTER TWENTY-ONE:

What the Mirror Remembers

The café was quiet for a Thursday afternoon.

Not empty—just reverent.

The kind of hush that settles only in places where people come to remember something, even if they don't know what it is.

She had chosen it deliberately—off the main street, tucked between a bookstore and a florist's shop.

The kind of place that smelled like old books and cinnamon, where no one asked your name but remembered your order.

It felt like grace in a paper cup.

Across from her sat Alma—retired teacher, unapologetic truth-teller, and accidental prophet.

A woman with soft hands and sharper vision, who wore her years like armor and her wisdom like perfume—quiet, but undeniable.

They met once a month. Sometimes more.

It started as mentorship.

Then friendship.

Now... something closer to confession.

Alma stirred her tea with a crooked spoon, the silver worn smooth from decades of stories.

She watched her companion over the rim of her glasses with eyes that saw more than they let on.

"You've been quiet today," she said, her voice low and lined with gravel. "Even for you."

The woman smiled faintly. "I've been thinking."

"Mm." Alma raised one eyebrow. "That's where most trouble begins."

She gave a soft laugh, but it didn't reach her chest.

Not today.

Alma tilted her head. "Is this about someone?"

A long pause. Then:

"Yes. A long time ago, I... left someone."

"Or something?" Alma asked, not unkindly.

She nodded. "Both."

She didn't give details.

Not at first.

Just fragments, spoken like loose thread from an old garment she was only now willing to mend.

"He was good. Steady. Too steady, maybe. And I... I needed more."

"More what?"

"I don't know. More... recognition? More noise? Something brighter, sharper, louder.

Something that made me feel important."

Alma didn't rush her.

That was her gift.

Silence without pressure.

Stillness that let truth rise on its own.

"I thought I wanted something bigger. Flashier. I wanted to matter."

She exhaled.

"And for a while… I did. I think I still do. But—" her fingers curled tightly around the warm ceramic mug— "I don't feel like I do."

Alma nodded slowly, like someone folding a sacred page.

"Did he love you?"

The woman's breath caught.

"Yes," she said.

Her voice almost broke.

"Like air. Like prayer. Like I was the answer to something he never asked aloud."

"And you left?"

"Yes."

Alma leaned back. Her face softened—not with pity, but recognition.

"Honey," she said slowly, "sometimes the richest lives don't look like much from the outside. And sometimes the most radiant hearts get overlooked until they're no longer beating."

The words didn't hit all at once.

They sank—like stones tossed into deep water.

And in her chest, they echoed like bells in an empty sanctuary.

"Why are you thinking of him now?" Alma asked, her voice gentler.

"I don't know," she began, then corrected herself:

"I do. I saw something. An article, a photo… it wasn't even of him. But it felt like it was.

Like the universe pulled back the curtain for just a moment and said, *Remember?*"

She paused.

Swallowed.

"It hit me in a place I thought had closed. And I realized…

I never honored him.

Not truly.

Not the way I should've."

Alma reached across the table and touched her hand. Her fingers were warm, dry, sure.

"Do you want to go back?" she asked.

She didn't answer right away.

The word *yes* hovered on her tongue but never landed.

"I want to know if I *could*," she said instead.

Alma held her gaze, still and steady. "And what if you're too late?"

She looked down, blinking hard.

"Then I want to at least… honor what I left.

I want him to know—I saw it.

I finally saw it."

They sat in silence after that.

Not the kind that asks to be broken,

but the kind that makes room for truth to stretch its legs.

Alma sipped her tea.

The woman watched the sky through the window—clouds shifting like memories across a canvas she couldn't repaint.

After a while, Alma whispered,

"Some souls come into our lives to anchor us, even if we drift. And sometimes… they don't wait for us to return.

They just… let go."

Tears gathered.

They didn't fall.

But they glistened.

She nodded.

Because some part of her already knew.

He wasn't waiting.
But he had never stopped giving.
And maybe that was the measure of his love—
Not in how long he held on,
but in how gently he let her go.

CHAPTER TWENTY-TWO:

The Widow's Letter

The letter wasn't long.

Just a quiet column in the back of the local paper—a half page nestled between church announcements and recipe swaps. You could've missed it.

Most did.

But for those who read carefully, it said more than any headline ever could.

Its title read simply:

> *"A Life Worth Noticing"*
> *By M. Delaney, Linwood Resident*

> *I don't often write to newspapers.*
> *And I certainly don't write obituaries.*
> *But I suppose this isn't one.*
> *Not really.*
> *It's a note.*
> *Of thanks.*
> *He was a quiet man.*
> *You'd pass him on the street and not think twice.*
> *Flannel shirt. Old boots. Always something growing on his hands—*
> *dirt, or calluses, or kindness.*

When my Henry passed, I couldn't figure out the stove.

Not the big one—the little one in the corner.

The one we used to warm water in the winter and make soup on cold evenings when our bones remembered their age.

I didn't call anyone.

Didn't cry.

Just stared at that stove like it had betrayed me.

Two days later, I came home from the market and it worked again.

No note.

No explanation.

Just the faint scent of tomato leaves still hanging in the air—like he'd passed through just moments before—and a prayer card resting neatly on the counter.

Folded once.

Blank on the back, except for a single word in his handwriting: Peace.

He never asked for thanks.

Never came back to check.

Just fixed what was broken and let silence finish the conversation.

I've baked bread every Tuesday since.

Ritual, I suppose.

Because kindness deserves ritual.

And maybe memory does too.

If you ask me, we lost a good man last month.

Not famous. Not loud.

But faithful.

And isn't that rarer these days?

Some folks make noise.

Others make space.

He made space.

For widows like me.
For children with questions.
For strangers too tired to knock.
He never preached.
But somehow, he taught us how to stay.
How to kneel without knees hitting the floor.
How to believe that quiet isn't weakness—it's strength surrendered.
I suppose saints don't always wear robes.
Maybe they wear flannel and carry tin cans.
Maybe they leave gardens instead of sermons.
Maybe they go unnoticed—until you realize the room is colder without them in it.
If you see his bench under the olive tree, sit down a while.
Let the stillness settle.
That's where he met the world.
Where he offered his faith one breath at a time.
He made space for people like us.
And he left that space behind, as gently as he lived.
With reverence,
—M. Delaney

She never saw the woman read it.
Never knew if she did.
But somewhere across the distance,
in a city apartment too polished for its own good,
fingers trembled slightly over a chipped coffee cup,
and a single line echoed in the hollow spaces between memory
and regret:

"Maybe saints wear flannel…"

And she closed her eyes.
Not in mourning.
But in recognition.
For what had been given,
and what had been lost.

CHAPTER TWENTY-THREE:
The Planting

It was still dark when he rose.

Not from obligation.

Not from restlessness.

But from a stirring too quiet to ignore. A whisper that lived deeper than thought, deeper than feeling. A call in the marrow.

The sky was a faded navy, just beginning to bleed light at its edges—the kind of hour when the world feels suspended, wrapped in the breath between dreams and daylight. No birds yet. No voices. Only the hush of everything waiting to be named.

In that holy pause, he moved through his modest home with the tenderness of someone who knew goodbyes didn't always knock. They often crept in through silence and settled like dust on the things you thought would stay.

He didn't dress with ceremony.

No polished shoes. No ironed shirt.

Only his soft flannel, worn thin at the elbows, and boots that still bore the press of yesterday's path. His movements were slow, deliberate—the kind of slowness that honors time, not escapes it.

The tin can sat on the kitchen table where he had left it the night before.

Waiting.

It was nothing special. A repurposed coffee tin, the kind that once sat on pantry shelves in simpler kitchens. It had been washed, dried, set aside—its label long peeled away, leaving only a faint ring of glue and memory. The ghost of convenience past, now made sacred by intention.

Inside, wrapped in a faded handkerchief that had once belonged to his father, was the ring.

Not extravagant. Not ornate.

Just gold—modest, honest, the kind of ring chosen by a man who believed love should speak plainly.

He hadn't planned on placing it there.

Not originally.

He had considered the box on the shelf, the drawer where he kept his keepsakes, even the pocket of a suit jacket he rarely wore. But none of those felt right. None of them breathed the kind of quiet reverence this act required.

It was the earth.

The tree.

The spot beneath the branches that had listened to so many of his prayers. That had watched him grieve, and give, and wait. That had kept still when she sat beside him for the last time, not knowing how much of him she would take when she left.

So he picked up the tin like a man carrying something fragile—not because it would break, but because it already held what was broken.

No letter.

No inscription.

No folded page to explain the ache or the offering.

Just the ring.

Simple. Humble. Born of sweat and sacrifice.

He had earned it mowing lawns, fixing fences, helping strangers for nothing but thanks and loaves of bread. He had chosen it carefully, not because it sparkled, but because it held quiet. The kind of quiet he hoped to share a life in.

He had once held it in his hand on the day she said goodbye.

He had stood in the doorway, heart braced, ring tucked in his palm, words gathered like petals on the edge of bloom.

But the question never came.

Or maybe it did—unspoken, hanging in the space between breath and hesitation.

And he, in his silence, chose not to ask.

Not because he lacked courage.

But because love, the kind he believed in, did not demand.

And now, love required something quieter still.

He walked the familiar path to the tree. The dew was thick on the grass, kissing his boots with each step. Fog clung low like an old wool blanket, draped across the land, softening everything it touched. The olive tree waited—its branches raised like arms in prayer, its roots tangled in stories only the soil remembered.

The bench sat still, half-swallowed by ivy. He knelt beside it. Not out of duty, but devotion.

He dug with his hands, letting the earth press beneath his fingernails, warm and damp and alive. It wasn't deep—just enough. Just a cradle for what he was about to let go.

He placed the tin can into the hollow, fitting it between roots like tucking something into the hands of a sleeping elder.

Then he covered it again. Slowly. Gently. With fingers that had built shelves, and held children, and cupped prayers. Fingers that trembled now—not from age, but from the weight of what he had chosen not to keep.

He sat back on his heels and pressed his palms flat against the soil.

Not grief.

Not hope.

Something holier.

A surrender.

A knowing that some seeds are not planted for harvest, but for memory. That some loves are not meant to be worn, but buried—in sacred places, beneath the shade of something that outlives them.

He stayed there a while.

Breathing.

Listening.

Letting the quiet say what his words could not.

Then he whispered—not with sound, but with presence.

A prayer not to be answered. Only heard.

And finally, he stood.

Not lighter.

But steadier.

His palms dusted with soil.

His heart emptied of asking.

And filled with peace.

And as the light finally broke across the hills, spilling warmth over the earth he had touched, he turned, and walked back the way he came—leaving behind the ring, the tin, the silence.

Leaving behind... love.

Planted. Rooted. Kept.

CHAPTER TWENTY-FOUR:

The Final Season

The days had grown quieter.
Not in the way winter hushes a town, but in the way the soul begins to soften before it leaves the body.

He could feel it—like the thinning of a veil, the gentling of breath, the way morning dew rests heavier on petals just before they fall.

He wasn't sick. Not exactly.

Just… tired.

Bone-tired.

The kind of tired that seeps into marrow, not from labor, but from the long and faithful carrying of years.

As though his spirit had been whispering goodbye long before his lips ever would.

He moved slower now, but not with sorrow.

With reverence.

Each step had grown more intentional. He no longer mistook time for something to race. He folded his shirts like he was remembering their weight. He swept the porch not just for tidiness, but to listen to the sound of bristles brushing across the past.

He did not count his days. He blessed them.

Even the silent ones.

Especially the silent ones.

The olive tree was in bloom.

Even now, in the slow dance of his last days, it stood tall—its roots tangled with memory, its branches shaped by prayers he never spoke aloud. Its bark carried echoes of conversations, of silent reckonings, of rings buried and dreams released.

He often sat beneath it, hands folded.

Not to ask for anything.

But to give thanks.

For breath.

For bread.

For the few who saw him.

And the One who always did.

The breeze would play in its leaves like a hymn, and sometimes, he thought he could hear the names of those he had loved rustling through them.

Some returned.

Most did not.

But the wind carried them all back, if only for a moment.

He did not curse the ache in his knees, the fog that sometimes clouded his memory, the quiet that grew louder with each passing day.

These were not burdens.

They were confirmations.

That he had lived fully, even when unnoticed.

He didn't speak of death.

He simply prepared.

There was no list to check off. No grand farewell.

Just small acts of final tending.

He mended the frayed rope at the well—not because he'd need it again, but because someone else might.

He repotted the herbs on the windowsill.

Sharpened the tools in the shed.

Left extra soup in the freezer with notes in careful handwriting: *If you need comfort, warm this slowly.*

He organized the contents of his small wooden chest—letters, tokens, a few coins worn soft by fingers that had given more than they'd ever held back.

And a photograph.

Just one.

Her face was barely visible in the background of a town picnic, laughing at something he couldn't quite remember. But he remembered the sound of her laughter.

He didn't frame it.

He just kept it.

Folded gently between the pages of his journal, beside scriptures marked in the corners with stars and smudges.

He dusted the bench beneath the tree one last time, pausing to trace its worn grain, to remember how many stories had passed through that seat.

How many had left different than they arrived.

In the evenings, he wrote.

Not for an audience.

Not for history.

But for her.

Still.

Not to woo.

Not to wound.

But to witness.

To say the things silence had once been asked to carry.

To tell the truth of love as he had known it—not love that clutched, or chased, or demanded.

But love that watched her leave and still lit a candle for her return.

*"You were the melody I never stopped humming,
even when the world around me fell quiet."*

His handwriting trembled in places now, the letters a little less sure. But the message?

Unwavering.

He folded the page and tucked it into the middle of the journal, pressing it there like a blessing between chapters.

The ink still wet with grace.

One night, beneath a sky too vast to measure, he left the door open.

Not for visitors.

For the wind.

He sat at the edge of his bed, a wool blanket pulled across his lap, looking out at the tree, the stars, the soft flicker of the candle he lit each night without fail.

The flame swayed gently.

The branches above shifted like breath.

The shadows on the floor moved as if the house itself was exhaling.

He let his thoughts wander—not in loops of longing, but in trails of peace. He remembered small hands pressed into his for guidance. Remembered the sound of his own laughter, rare but real. Remembered the taste of tomatoes in summer. The hush of shared tea. The scent of rosemary.

And in that quiet moment, he closed his eyes—

—not in fear.

But in fulfillment.

Not because everything had turned out the way he once dreamed.

But because he had turned into the kind of man who didn't need it to.

The next morning, the neighbors noticed the smoke had not risen from his chimney.

The well had gone untouched.

The garden unswept.

The birds still came, but the seed tray lay empty.

Mrs. Everson knocked first.

Then again.

And when there was no answer, she stepped inside.

They found him as they hoped they would—

not slumped, not in pain.

But at rest.

Peaceful.

Hands resting on his chest.

The blue tie still knotted gently at his throat—the one she had given him all those years ago, still crisp at the edges, still honored.

Beside him lay his journal, opened to a final entry, the ink still dark and sure:

> *"If love never returned to me,*
> *it is only because it never left."*

They buried him beneath the olive tree.

No grand procession.

No formal eulogies.

Just the wind.

The birds.

The pages of his journal, folded neatly inside a tin box, placed beneath a weathered bench he once built with bare hands and gentle purpose.

The same bench where she once sat.

Where the boy had eaten tomatoes.

Where the elder left a loaf of warm bread.

And the tie—still around his neck.

Still keeping time.

Not with seconds.

But with love.

Later that evening, just as the sun sank behind the chapel roof, Alma approached the tree.

She moved without ceremony, her shawl pulled close around her shoulders, her steps careful but assured.

In her hand, a small sprig of rosemary. Or maybe basil. She never told anyone. She knelt, briefly, and tucked it into the softened soil between the roots where the ivy parted just enough to receive it. Just above where the tin lay hidden.

"For remembrance," she whispered. "For healing. For peace."

And then she stood, eyes misty but calm, and walked away without looking back.

A breeze rustled through the branches, lifting the scent of rosemary into the morning air.

CHAPTER TWENTY-FIVE:

The Search Begins

She couldn't sleep.

It was the third night in a row that the ceiling held more comfort than the bed, and the moonlight seemed to whisper things she didn't want to hear. Shadows crawled gently along the plaster walls like thoughts too polite to wake her fully, but too persistent to let her rest.

She tossed the blanket aside. Walked barefoot across the hardwood floor, its chill familiar but grounding. The city outside kept humming—streetlights blinking in rhythm with late-night taxis and dreams bought on credit. But her thoughts had wandered elsewhere.

His name hadn't been spoken aloud in years.

Not in conversation.

Not even in confession.

But now, it hovered at the edge of every thought.

Not his full name. Not yet.

Just the memory of his voice.

The cadence of his quiet.

And the silence he left behind when she walked away.

Not angry silence.

Not bitter.

Just... still.

The kind that lingered even after the door had closed.

It began innocently enough.

A moment of avoidance disguised as productivity.

She opened her laptop to search for a contract, a file buried in a maze of digital folders. Her eyes skimmed, mechanical, until something stopped her.

An old folder.

Long untouched.

Inside it—an unsent draft.

Subject line: *I was wrong.*

No message.

No greeting.

Just the date. Five years ago.

She didn't remember writing it.

Couldn't recall the moment her fingers hovered over the keys but never pressed send.

But it felt like her.

The her that still carried questions.

The her that had stopped looking for answers but never stopped wondering.

She stared at it for a long while, cursor blinking like a heartbeat.

She didn't open it.

Didn't delete it either.

Just let it be.

As though it, too, was waiting.

Later that day, she passed a bookstore.

She hadn't meant to go in. Was on her way to meet a friend for coffee, or maybe she was avoiding another networking lunch. But the display in the window made her stop.

A notebook. Simple. Leather-bound.

Not flashy. Not branded.

Just familiar.

Not unlike the one he always carried—creased at the spine, soft around the edges, full of silence and scribbled prayers.

She stepped inside.

Not for the notebook.

But for something else.

Something she couldn't name.

Toward the back, past the glossy fiction and overpriced candles, she found a shelf stacked with old local publications— free weeklies, church bulletins, community magazines with names like *The Bell Tower* and *Neighborly Notes*.

She ran her fingers along their edges, not expecting anything.

But there it was.

Near the back of one.

A photo.

Grainy. Small.

But unmistakable.

Him.

Standing beneath the olive tree.

His frame slightly bowed, hands in his pockets, chin lifted toward something the camera hadn't captured.

He hadn't changed much.

A little grayer, maybe.

A little thinner.

But still him.

Still steady.

Still peaceful.

The caption read:

A Man of Quiet Faith — Living Simply, Loving Deeply.

Her breath caught.

There was no name.

No byline.

Just a short tribute from a local editor.

Dated two months ago.

Panic didn't rise.

Only stillness.

A kind of reverence that comes when you realize the clock has kept ticking even while your heart stood still.

She purchased the magazine, though the cashier raised an eyebrow at the outdated cover. She didn't explain. Just smiled faintly and left.

At home, she laid it on the table like scripture.

She traced the photo with her finger, slow and reverent, as though it might dissolve if she pressed too hard.

Then she whispered, soft enough that even the walls wouldn't echo it:

"Where are you?"

It wasn't a demand.

It was a plea.

Or maybe a prayer.

That night, she dreamed of him.

He didn't speak.

He just sat beside her.

Hands folded.

That small, knowing smile he always wore—half peace, half ache.

The bench beneath him was empty.

No journal.

No bag.

Just the wind, and the sound of leaves shifting like breath.

The tree behind him swayed gently, branches catching moonlight like lace.

When she reached for him, he turned—not in sadness. But in peace.

And said, "You found me late.

But you still found me."

Then he was gone.

The tree remained.

And the wind kept humming the shape of his name.

She woke before dawn.

Tears had dried on her cheeks, unnoticed in the night.

The room felt heavier.

Or maybe it was lighter.

Like something had shifted just enough to matter.

She sat at the edge of her bed, not moving. Just breathing. And then, without ceremony, she stood.

She made tea.

She packed a bag.

She didn't call anyone.

Didn't explain.

There was no one who would understand in the way she needed.

She folded the magazine and tucked it between a scarf and a notebook. Not the old one. A new one. Still empty.

But not for long.

She would find the town again.

The tree.

The truth.

Not to reclaim what was lost.

But to touch it.

To sit with it.

To say, at last, without rushing:

"I saw you."

Even if only once more

CHAPTER TWENTY-SIX:
The Olive Tree Knows

I have stood here longer than most things.
Longer than pews and windows. Longer than promises.
Before the benches, before the children with their wild laughter and scraped knees, before the sorrow learned how to sit still—I was.

My bark has worn the years like a shawl of seasons, soft in places, stubborn in others.
They come and go, these people.
With their loud beginnings and quiet endings.
With their hands full of dreams and their hearts too afraid to open them.

But he—
He stayed.

He never carved his name into me.
Never laid flowers. Never asked for signs.
He just came.

He came when the sun was kind, and when it wasn't.
He came when the wind stilled, and when it howled like grief.
And when he sat at my roots,
he let the silence speak.

Not every man can do that.
Most fill the quiet with noise.

But he—he let the quiet teach him.
And I, in return, listened.

I've seen the girl, too.

The one with questions written behind her eyes—sharp, shimmering things that never quite found a home.

She used to laugh here once,
though she didn't realize how rare that sound was.
Like wind through glass.
Like grace in motion.

He noticed.

He always noticed.

She left.

But not all of her.

Some people leave shadows behind
the way others leave footprints.

The memory of her lingered in the breeze long after she was gone.
In the way the soil turned softer for a while.
In how he sat a little closer to me.

As though trying to hold space for something he knew he could not keep.

Still, he stayed.
Even when the air changed.
Even when hope dimmed to a whisper.

When he came with the ring,
he didn't bury it like grief.

He planted it.

Like belief.

Not with desperation.

Not with ceremony.

Just with quiet conviction.

No fanfare.

No farewell.

Just a man offering what was never accepted
to a future he would never see.

The earth took it gently.

It didn't resist.

And I—

I have kept it.

Wrapped it in root and rain.

Held it like a story not yet finished.

Because sometimes, love is not meant to be worn.

Sometimes, it is meant to be remembered.

To be sown.

To become.

I do not speak in words.

But I remember.

I remember the way his prayers moved through the roots,
not loud, but true.

I remember the way his heart broke without shattering,
the way he stitched grace into every morning like thread through
worn cloth.

I remember the pages he left tucked beneath the bench,
the ones only the wind and I read.

Lines written for no one.

But meant for someone.

And now—

She returns.

Older.

Softer.

Searching.

She does not yet know what she's searching for.

She thinks it is him.

His face. His voice. Some relic of who he was.

But really,

she has come to find herself

in the place he last believed

she might still bloom.

She will kneel.

She will weep.

She will ask the ground questions it cannot answer.

And when her hands touch the soil,

I will loosen—just enough.

Not all at once.

Not everything.

But enough.

The ring.

The page.

The pieces of love

that never had to be loud to be true.

I will offer them—not as proof.

But as blessing.

And I will cover them again.

Not to hide.

But to remind:

That love, when rooted, does not rot.

It does not vanish.

It does not demand a witness to be real.

It becomes the earth it was buried in.

And grows again.

CHAPTER TWENTY-SEVEN:

The Road Back

The highway stretched out like a long-held breath.

A ribbon of gray winding between hills that once held her dreams loosely, like petals waiting for wind.

She hadn't driven this road in over a decade, yet it remembered her.

Not with signs or announcements—just with rhythm.

Every turn, every pine-laced silence whispered pieces of a past she'd tucked away in suitcases and speeches and glittering rooms filled with people who never asked who she used to be.

She drove with the windows cracked just enough to let the wind in.

Not enough to muss her hair—

but enough to remember.

The scent of earth after morning rain.

The hum of cicadas growing louder as the day warmed.

The way stillness sounded different out here—less like emptiness, more like invitation.

She wasn't ready for what waited at the end of the road.

But she had already begun.

And that was something.

The fields were still there.

That same patch of wildflowers danced along the hillside, defiantly alive, indifferent to her return.

The old red barn sagged a little more than before, weathered but proud, like an elder who'd stopped minding the vanity of repair.

Even the crooked sign at the town entrance remained—its white paint flaked like time itself had been trying to peel it away letter by letter.

Welcome to Linwood. Population: Unknown.

She smiled, though her chest ached.
Funny how one word—*welcome*—could feel like both grace and grief at once.

It was strange, returning not as a lover or a resident, but as a visitor to a life she once considered hers.

A ghost walking the borders of a memory,
hoping something still lived there.
Hoping something still recognized her.

She passed the old general store.

The bell above the door still jingled as a man stepped out with a brown paper bag tucked against his ribs.

He didn't look her way.

No one did.

That was the gift of small towns.

And sometimes, its sorrow.

You could disappear into them without trying.
And sometimes, you did.

She drove slowly past places that had no reason to hold her name anymore—

the worn gazebo, the faded mural by the schoolyard, the gravel road that led to a now-empty field where he once taught her to see constellations with her bare eyes and open trust.

Everything looked smaller.

Or maybe she had grown too tall in the wrong ways.

Too polished.

Too practiced.

Too late.

She parked near the church but didn't go in.

Not yet.

The chapel steeple still touched the sky with its same quiet posture—not proud, just present.

She walked instead.

Past the post office with its slanted box and fading notices.

Past the creek where he once skipped stones in that patient, childlike way of his, whispering stories he never finished.

Past the café where they shared their first awkward silence— back when silence wasn't heavy,
just new.

Back when being known still felt possible.

The world here had not paused for her absence.

Nor had it punished her for it.

It had simply gone on.

As kind places often do.

She paused outside the house.

His house.

Modest. Neatly kept.

The porch swept clean, as if still expecting guests who never knocked.

No car in the drive.

No footprints in the dust.

A curtain stirred in the window.

But no one was there.

She didn't approach.

She couldn't.

Not yet.

Not while her hands still trembled with questions.

Not while her heart still measured distance in regrets.

By afternoon, the clouds rolled in.

Not storming—just watching.

The kind of sky that holds its tears the way old friends hold secrets.

She found a bench near the garden behind the chapel.

Sat down. Exhaled.

The kind of exhale that only comes after years of pretending you never held your breath.

The kind that empties everything at once—ambition, noise, pretending.

And that's when she saw it.

The tree. Olive. Old. Knowing.

She rose slowly, feet crunching gravel, heart unsure of what it would find.

But her soul…her soul knew.

As she neared, something shifted.

Not the wind.

Not the light.

Her.

Something inside her unfastened.

Unbuckled.

Unbound.

The place remembered her.

Even if she had forgotten how to belong.

She reached the tree—and there it was.

A small weathered stone, nestled in grass, bathed in late afternoon hush.

No name carved into grandeur.

Just five words etched into the base:

"He *loved without needing return.*"

She covered her mouth.

And wept.

Not loudly.

But fully.

The kind of weeping that doesn't ask to be comforted.

Only witnessed.

The kind of grief that is rooted in beauty.

In mercy.

In missed things that still offered grace.

Next to the bench, tucked beneath its wooden slats, was a tin box.

She didn't touch it yet.

Not because she was afraid of what was inside.

But because she already knew.

It was him.

What remained.

What never left.

What waited—

not for her return…

…but for her recognition.

Chapter Twenty-Eight:

What Was Always There

The journal was warm from the sun.

She held it in her lap, fingers resting lightly on the leather cover, as if afraid her touch might erase what time had preserved.

Its edges were weather-soft, corners rounded not by carelessness, but by frequent holding—like something not often shown, but always returned to.

Birdsong circled the branches above.

The olive tree swayed with slow remembrance,

leaves whispering in a language older than grief.

Insects hummed without apology.

A breeze brushed the tall grass like a lullaby with no words.

The world did not know this was a holy moment.

And neither, fully, did she.

Not yet.

She opened the cover.

No preamble.

No "Dear anyone."

Just a date, faintly written in the corner—

years ago.

The first page bled with ink and restraint,

as though each word had cost him something to place there.

"Today I saw her again.

She didn't see me.
But she moved like she used to.
Confident. Distant.
The kind of beautiful that doesn't know it is.
I almost waved.
But I remembered: I'd already said goodbye.
Some goodbyes are spoken with absence, not words."

Her breath caught.
Not in drama.
In recognition.
This wasn't nostalgia.
This was presence.
She turned the page.

"They say the heart doesn't break—
it just bends until it reshapes itself around the empty space.
If that's true, then I suppose mine has grown new edges."

She paused.
Her thumb brushed the edge of the page like a blessing
Something stirred.
A distant echo,
like a door unlatching in her mind.
The handwriting.
The cadence.
The way he always used to pause at truth like it was a cliff's edge.
No. Not yet.
She turned the page again.

"I heard her name today.
Not from her lips,
but from someone asking if I knew what became of her.
I didn't answer.
How could I?
I've known her in ways the world never will,
and yet I don't know where she sleeps,
what dreams she keeps,
or if she remembers the sound of my voice."

She closed her eyes.
It was him.
And this—
This was his voice.

Not just in pen and page,
but in rhythm,
in reverence,
in restraint.

Her hands trembled.
Not from shock.
But from memory.

From every moment she had pushed aside the truth:
That he had waited.

Not at a door.
Not in bitterness.
Not in foolish hope.
But in spirit.
In kindness.
In the unwavering stillness of someone
who loved without needing return.

A quiet sound escaped her lips.
Not quite a sob.
Not quite a prayer.
Something softer.
Like grace.
Like recognition.
She turned to the final page.

"If she ever returns,
I won't ask why she left.
I'll only thank the heavens for her shadow
passing once more across the doorway of this quiet life.
I loved her as I was taught to love:
with nothing held back.
And if no one ever knows,
that's all right.
The tree will."

Her breath stopped—
just for a moment—
as if the air itself had paused to make room
for the weight of it all.
The journal slid gently from her hands.
She didn't catch it.
Didn't need to.
It landed softly in her lap.
Like trust.
Like closure that didn't close.
She leaned back against the bench,
eyes closed,

head tilted to the sky
as the olive leaves whispered above.
     And in that breathless moment,
something aligned.
Not in name.
Not in certainty.
But in memory—
the kind that lives in fingertips and silence.
     She stayed there for hours.
Not reading anymore.
Just being.
     She didn't weep for the years.
Not now.
     She didn't regret her return—
only that she had taken so long to begin it.
     She simply listened.
To the rustling above.
To the heartbeat beneath the soil.
To the man who had always spoken in silence.
     And finally,
finally,
she heard him.

CHAPTER TWENTY-NINE:
What Remains

She came back one more time.
Not for answers.
Not for closure.
Just to sit.
Just to be.
To breathe where he once breathed.
To place herself in the stillness that once shaped him.

It was early morning—the kind of hush that drapes the world in soft gold and birdsong.

The town still hadn't woken, but the olive tree had. Its leaves lifted in the breeze, as if nodding in welcome, as if it knew her shape before she ever reached the bench.

She wore no makeup.

No jewelry.

A plain cardigan and jeans that didn't quite fit like they used to.

There was a softness in her step now— not fragility, but surrender.

Her hair was pinned back.

Her heart, unguarded.

She carried a small paper sack tucked beneath her arm,

creased at the corner from having been held too tightly for too long.

She sat on the same bench.

The one where she had found the journal.

The one where his words had begun to unspool her carefully constructed life.

She didn't reread it.

She didn't need to.

She had memorized enough.

A phrase here. A line there.

A breath where he once paused.

A truth she'd once refused.

A weightless kind of love,
now pressed into the folds of her memory
like dried lavender between pages.

She closed her eyes,
let the stillness wrap around her like a shawl, and she might have stayed in that moment longer—
had she not heard the soft crunch of footsteps approaching the garden path.

She turned.

A young man stood a few paces away.

Tall.

Sun-warmed.

His hands bore the calluses of someone who worked the land.

His eyes—
carried something steady—
something she hadn't seen in years.

A recognition of the place

Though he didn't speak at first,

something unspoken passed between them.

He looked at the tree.

Then the journal.

Then her.

"I'm sorry," he said gently. "I didn't mean to intrude."

"You're not," she said.

"This place… I used to come here when I was a boy."

She blinked.

"You knew him?"

The young man stepped closer, just enough to glimpse the journal resting beside her and the soft paper sack folded gently in her lap—

like something waiting to be offered or buried.

He nodded toward the journal. "He used to write in that almost every morning."

She followed his gaze, her eyes softening.

"I remember," she said, her voice quiet but sure. "Every page felt like him."

The young man smiled gently, then glanced toward the garden. "I was just a kid when he taught me how to plant tomatoes back here."

She stared at him, surprised.

"I didn't talk much back then," he continued.

"Didn't know how to grieve.

But he didn't need me to explain.

He just handed me a trowel and let the garden do the listening."

She swallowed the ache in her throat.

"What was he like? To you?"

"He let me work in the garden," he said. "Never asked why I showed up—just handed me the trowel like I belonged here."

He glanced down, smiled faintly.

"He taught me how to wait. That was his real gift, I think. He let things take root without forcing them to grow."

She looked at him fully now, something welling in her eyes that she didn't try to hide.

"He changed you."

He nodded.

"And you?"

She held his gaze, then looked down at her palms, still dusted with soil.

"He waited for me to see what I couldn't back then."

For a while, neither spoke.

Then the young man reached into his canvas bag and pulled out a single ripe tomato.

"I bring one every time," he said with a shy grin.

"Still tastes like summers and stories."

He handed it to her.

She held it like a relic.

A gift passed down through hands that had once held hope.

He stepped back.

"Take your time," he said. "He'd have wanted that."

She nodded, unable to find words.

He gave a quiet smile—

the kind that didn't ask for anything in return.

The young man looked toward the porch, where the wind moved gently through the screen door.

"He never asked for anything," he said. "Just gave.

And somehow, for some reason, I welcomed everything he had to give. Although I didn't really know its true value until years later."

The moment stood in a stillness that felt holy.

The young man looked toward the porch, where the wind moved gently through the screen door.

"He never asked for anything," he said. "Just gave.

And somehow, for some reason, I welcomed everything he had to give.

Although I didn't really know its true value until years later."

He paused. Not to linger, but to honor the quiet.

The kind of pause you give before leaving a place that shaped you.

His gaze returned to her, warm and steady.

"I'm glad you came back," he said. "He would've been too."

She nodded, unable to speak past the ache blooming behind her ribs.

He took a slow step back, the gravel crunching softly beneath his boots.

Then another.

"Take care," he said, and this time it wasn't just a farewell—

It was a benediction.

A blessing left between two strangers bound by the same root.

She watched him go.

Not with longing.

But with reverence.

His steps were slow and unhurried, like someone who knew the way by heart.

She remained still,

letting the silence settle again.

A silence that had been shared—
now returned to her alone.

The air felt different somehow.
Not emptier,
but fuller.
Like something had been passed on, quietly, without ceremony.

The journal fluttered in the wind as it rested beside her.

The tomato cradled gently in her palm.

And somewhere deep within—
beneath guilt, beneath grief, beneath all the words she never said—
something softened.
Something opened.
Something remained.

She sat with it.

Not the young man's words, nor even the memory of the man they both had loved—
but the echo of both, gently braided into the stillness.
Not everything needed to be said aloud.
Some stories finished their telling in the soil.

She had brought a small trowel
but found herself using her hands instead—
cupping the soil, pulling it back gently
the way one might draw back a blanket from a sleeping child.

She worked slowly, almost reverently.
The morning sun barely lifted the mist, which haloed around the olive tree's crooked limbs like breath around a miracle.

The earth was softer than expected.

The soil gave easily beneath her fingers—as though it, too, had been waiting.

She had carried the tomato seeds in a brown envelope, folded twice and worn at the creases.

They had been tucked in the drawer beside the kitchen sink—long forgotten or perhaps too sacred to use until now.

Small. Ordinary. Tomato seeds.

The kind he used to grow behind his house.

The kind she once mocked lightly—called them "peasant fruit" at a dinner party, back when laughter cost less than respect.

He had only smiled, said nothing, and served her the ripest one with a pinch of sea salt and an old spoon shaped by time.

She hadn't forgotten.

Not really.

Not the taste.

Not the way his silence sometimes said more than any clever remark ever could.

It wasn't grief that brought her back.
Not entirely.

It was something quieter.
A kind of listening.

A wish, maybe, to tend to something she never gave a chance to grow.

She reached into the sack.

Pulled out the seeds and emptied them into the palm of her hands as though to touch the moment one last time.

As she pressed the seeds into the soil—three at a time, spaced the way he used to do—

her fingers brushed against something solid beneath the earth.

Not a root.

Not a stone.

She stilled.

Brushed the dirt away until a small rusted tin can emerged, its lid still intact.

It opened with a soft metallic pop,
and inside she found a box.

Velvet. Faded. Weathered.
Time-warmed like something cherished once,
and then released.

Time slowed.

She didn't gasp.
She didn't look around.

She knew—
somehow, she had always known—
that his love had gone deeper than words,
deeper even than his silence.

She opened the box.

A ring.
Simple. Modest. Clean.

It glinted with a memory that never got made.
Shimmered like it had been waiting
for a question that never got asked.

He was going to ask her.
He was going to propose a forever-life with her.

And she had already chosen something else.
She had chosen everything the world said would matter—
and lost what only the quiet can keep.

She didn't cry.
She didn't wear it.
She didn't whisper regrets into the wind.

She simply held it there,

its gold reflecting a thousand things she would never be able to say.

She held it for a while— felt its weight, not in gold, but in all the hours it must have taken him to believe she might say yes.

She ran her thumb along the band, then gently placed it back inside the can. She returned it to the earth.

Tamped the soil closed— as if tucking it in for one final sleep. Like it was a sacred promise.

Then she sat beside it, beneath the tree, and listened.

Her palms dusted with the scent of newness Her breath slowed to match the rhythm of roots.

It wasn't an apology.

It wasn't a tribute.

It was simply…remembrance.

A breeze stirred through the olive branches, soft and slow, like someone whispering a song too familiar to forget.

A hymn with no chorus—just memory,
and mercy,
and the sound of what could've been.

Then she noticed it.

Just inside the split in the trunk—nearly hidden,
weathered into the grain—was a page.
Folded once, creased and fragile.

Paper softened by time,
but still intact.

She reached for it.

The ink was faded but readable,
the handwriting steady and unhurried—his.

The Last Seed

I did not live loudly.
I did not love famously.
I did not leave behind riches or monuments
or names carved in bold.
But I left seeds.
A few.
Quietly sown in soft places—
in the look I gave instead of the word,
in the forgiveness I offered before it was asked,
in the prayer no one heard but Heaven.
I have learned that love is not proven by how it ends,
but by how it endures when no one's watching.
If you found this page,
it means you stayed long enough
to notice what was buried—
not to be hidden,
but to be rooted.
And maybe, in some small way…so were you.

The sun climbed.
The bench warmed.
She didn't cry.
She didn't pray.
She just closed her eyes and let the breeze carry away
whatever lingered too long inside her.
And when she finally stood, it was not with certainty.
It was with stillness.

The kind that follows a soul finally pausing long enough to feel what it's tried not to.

She folded the page, placed it gently back into the crevice of the tree, and pressed her palm against the bark—
steady,
still.

Then she rose.

Left the seeds to the soil,
the ring to its resting place,
and the wind to carry what words could not.

And with nothing but silence around her,
she walked back down the path.

She didn't look back.
She didn't have to.

What remained, remained.

The tree behind her stood still.
Waiting.
Watching.
Rooted.

And some roots don't need to be seen to be known.

EPILOGUE:

Beneath the Olive Tree

The city lights blinked back at her as the car slid into its usual spot beneath the glass tower.

Familiar concrete.

Familiar doorman.

Familiar silence as the elevator opened to the penthouse suite.

She stepped inside—heels muffled by imported rugs, the hush of curated air brushing her shoulders like memory might.

She walked in, dropped her keys in the blue ceramic bowl by the door,

and exhaled into the curated stillness.

Everything was exactly as she left it.

Exactly.

Minimalist art. Dried lavender. The low hum of climate control.

Even the glass vase on the mantel hadn't tilted.

Except her.

And even that, she refused to admit.

Not yet.

She had returned from the town two days ago.

No press.

No story.

No one noticed her absence—not in the circles that measured worth by appearance, and certainly not in the inboxes flooded with requests for her insight, her voice, her presence.

She told no one where she went.
Said she needed air. A retreat. A clearing of the mind.
Words that were true in theory.

In truth, she had needed to stand beneath that olive tree and not collapse.

She had needed to feel the weight of roots.

To be confronted by silence that didn't ask her to explain herself.

She had needed to read his words and feel them press against her ribs like something once lost, now whispering,
"I never left."

She had needed to see her own absence etched into the soil— not in blame,
but in memory.

And now,
she needed to forget.
Or pretend to.

Pretend long enough for the city to reclaim her.

On the coffee table,
among art books and awards,
sat a small folded newspaper clipping.

Not even centered.
Not even flattened.

She'd saved it.
She didn't know why.
She hadn't meant to keep it.

Obituary:
Local Man Remembered for Quiet Acts of Kindness

No photo.
No accolades.
Just a few words.
His name barely noticed.
    She told herself she kept it for nostalgia.
    Not guilt.
Not grief.
Certainly not love.
    Just a nod to what was,
not what might have been.
    She poured a glass of wine and turned on the music.
Something classical.
Polished.
Emotionally sterile—
a string quartet trained not to feel too much.
    She sat.
She sipped.
She stared out over the skyline.
    Reminded herself that this—
this curated elegance, this sleek loneliness—
was the life she chose.
    And there was no room here for men
who grew tomatoes in the back garden
and gave the best parts of themselves
without asking anything in return.
    She told herself he would've been lonely here.
    She told herself he didn't really understand her world.

She told herself
he hadn't loved her as much as she remembered.
    And maybe,
if she told herself enough times,
it would become true.
    Maybe.
    Somewhere far away,
beneath the olive tree,
the wind moved gently through the branches.
    No name carved.
No stone polished.
No grand legacy left behind.
    But he remained there.
    Not in body.
But in the way stories linger when no one speaks them aloud.
In the way truth makes itself known,
even if no one admits it.
    In the quiet, rooted memory of a man
who never needed applause to believe he mattered.
    In her penthouse,
she opened her laptop.
    The world was waiting—
her next speech,
her next column,
her next curated moment of importance.
    Deadlines blinked in digital font.
Notifications buzzed at the edges of her screen like flies.
    And yet—
    Somewhere between keystrokes,
a voice rose up from beneath the soil of her spirit.

Soft.
Steady.
Unrelenting.

"You were loved.
Not because of who you became.
But because of who you were...
when you were still becoming."

She froze.
Not from fear.
But from recognition.
Like hearing a hymn you didn't know you remembered.
She closed the laptop.
Gently.
As though it might shatter.
She looked out over the city again.
Glass towers.
Red taillights.
People chasing what they might never name.
And she said nothing.
Because there was nothing left to say.
Only one thing remained.
A memory,
still humming beneath her skin.
A bench beneath a tree.
A journal folded beside a heart that never closed.
A ring buried in love, not in loss.
And the wind,
still moving through the branches,

as if brushing against her shoulder—
reminding her:

Some things are never truly left behind.
They just grow roots
where only the quiet
can reach them.

And as she stepped back into the city's hum, one quiet sentence from that journal followed her, humming like breath beneath the noise:

"I never intended to leave a legacy. Only a life."

She smiled.
Because it remained, as it always had.
Not perfect. Not resolved. But held.
And that—unspoken, steady—was its own kind of answer.

~ ~ ~

She never told anyone about the seeds.

But somewhere, in the soft crease of a new journal,
her pen began again.

Not to explain.
Just to remember.

And in another town—maybe far, maybe not
—someone else will find their own
quiet place beneath a tree,
pick up what was left behind,
and begin reading.

Because love, once rooted, has a way of returning
in new names,
in new hands,
in new pages.

Afterword and Invitation

"Stories don't end when the pages close—they echo in conversations, in questions, in the quiet spaces between strangers who suddenly understand each other." —J. D. Smith

Acknowledgments

To the ones who listen quietly—thank you for understanding stories that don't shout.

To every reader who has ever been passed by, overlooked, or loved in silence—this was written with you in mind.

To my early readers, friends, and kind-hearted believers: your encouragement was a porch light left on. You know who you are.

To those who have taught me what love looks like when it isn't asked to perform—your legacy is in every sentence.

And finally,
to the One who sees even the smallest seeds,
who stays when we wander,
and who whispers through olive branches when we are still
enough to hear—

All of this was planted in the quiet
You have sown within our hearts.
May it take root,
and may it grow gently,
bearing fruit in seasons yet unseen.

READING GROUP GUIDE

For Book Clubs &

Gentle Conversations

What do you think the man meant when he wrote, "I never intended to leave a legacy. Only a life"? How does this idea challenge modern views on legacy and success?

1. The woman in the story is never named. How did this affect your reading of her? Did you see yourself in her?
2. Which moment or line stayed with you most? Why?
3. Discuss the theme of *stillness* throughout the book. What role does it play in healing, regret, and memory?
4. What does the olive tree represent for different characters? For you as a reader?
5. Do you think love that goes unspoken or unreturned still has meaning?
6. Would the story have changed for you if the man and woman had reunited before his death? Why or why not?
7. What was the role of faith in the man's life—and was it different from traditional portrayals of religious devotion?

8. The journal serves almost as a second character in the book. What do you think journals (or personal writings) offer that spoken words do not?

9. If you could write a letter to either character, what would you say?

10. Throughout the story, multiple characters "leave" something behind—seeds, notes, silence, prayers, a ring. Which of these gestures felt most meaningful to you, and why? What do you think the story is saying about legacy through these acts?

Prefer a printable copy?
Download the full Reader's Group Guide at:
www.scribeandcanvas.com/resources

Connect with the Author

To learn more about the upcoming series connected to *Beneath the Olive Tree*—as well as J. D. Smith's poetry and reflections on quiet faith, unseen love, and sacred memory—visit:

Website: www.scribeandcanvas.com

You can also sign up for journal letters, behind-the-scenes updates, and early release notes.

Because the stories that stay are often the ones whispered beneath the noise.